J. T. EDSON'S
FLOATING OUTFIT

The toughest bunch of Rebels that ever lost a war, they fought for the South, and then for Texas, as the legendary Floating Outfit of "Ole Devil" Hardin's O.D. Connected ranch.

MARK COUNTER was the best-dressed man in the West: always dressed fit-to-kill. BELLE BOYD was as deadly as she was beautiful, with a "Manhattan" model Colt tucked under her long skirts. THE YSABEL KID was Comanche fast and Texas tough. And the most famous of them all was DUSTY FOG, the ex-cavalryman known as the Rio Hondo Gun Wizard.

J. T. Edson has captured all the excitement and adventure of the raw frontier in this magnificent Western series. Turn the page for a complete list of Berkley Floating Outfit titles.

J. T. EDSON'S
FLOATING OUTFIT
WESTERN ADVENTURES
FROM BERKLEY

THE YSABEL KID

SET TEXAS BACK ON HER FEET

THE HIDE AND TALLOW MEN

TROUBLED RANGE

SIDEWINDER

McGRAW'S INHERITANCE

THE BAD BUNCH

TO ARMS, TO ARMS, IN DIXIE!

HELL IN THE PALO DURO

GO BACK TO HELL

THE SOUTH WILL RISE AGAIN

.44 CALIBER MAN

A HORSE CALLED MOGOLLON

GOODNIGHT'S DREAM

FROM HIDE AND HORN

THE HOODED RIDERS

QUIET TOWN

TRAIL BOSS

WAGONS TO BACKSIGHT

RANGELAND HERCULES

THE HALF BREED

THE WILDCATS

THE FAST GUNS

GUNS IN THE NIGHT

CUCHILO

A TOWN CALLED YELLOWDOG

THE TROUBLE BUSTERS

THE LAW OF THE GUN

THE PEACEMAKERS

THE RUSHERS

THE QUEST FOR BOWIE'S BLADE

THE FORTUNE HUNTERS

THE TEXAN

THE RIO HONDO KID

RIO GUNS

GUN WIZARD

TRIGGER FAST

RETURN TO BACKSIGHT

THE MAKING OF A LAWMAN

TERROR VALLEY

APACHE RAMPAGE

THE RIO HONDO WAR

THE FLOATING OUTFIT

THE MAN FROM TEXAS

GUNSMOKE THUNDER

THE SMALL TEXAN

THE TOWN TAMERS

WHITE INDIANS

OLD MOCCASINS ON THE TRAIL

WACO'S DEBT

THE HARD RIDERS

THE GENTLE GIANT

THE TRIGGER MASTER

THE TEXAS ASSASSIN

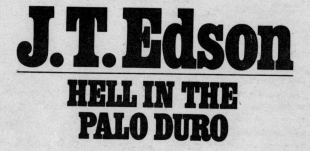

J. T. Edson

HELL IN THE PALO DURO

BERKLEY BOOKS, NEW YORK

HELL IN THE PALO DURO

A Berkley Book / published by arrangement with
Transworld Publishers, Ltd.

PRINTING HISTORY
Corgi edition published 1971
Berkley edition / October 1979
Fourth printing / October 1986

ISBN: 0-425-09361-1

A BERKLEY BOOK ® TM 757,375
Berkley Books are published by The Berkley Publishing Group,
200 Madison Avenue, New York, NY 10016.
The name "BERKLEY" and the stylized "B" with design
are trademarks belonging to Berkley Publishing Corporation.

PRINTED IN THE UNITED STATES OF AMERICA

For everybody who attended the 1970
Corgi Books Salesman of the Year
dinner. In the sincere hope that your
hangovers were as bad as mine.

CHAPTER ONE

DON'T COME AFTER ME

The Ysabel Kid, Waco and Sheriff Ian Laurie agreed that there were several puzzling aspects about the way in which the Glover gang had been acting since robbing the bank in Wichita Falls.

It was not so much the fact that Andy Glover had quit his normal hunting grounds in Eastern Texas. Having received orders from Governor Stanton Howard, the Texas Rangers had launched a vigorous campaign to stamp out the lawlessness which was flourishing in the Lone Star State. Naturally the owlhoots in the more civilized eastern counties were the first to feel the pressure.

Nor was there too much of a surprise in discovering that, having brought off a successful robbery, except for the loss of one man, the gang did not cover the twenty or so miles to the Red River to cross into the Indian Nations. Working in conjunction with the Texas Rangers, the Army and U.S. marshals planned to run out the outlaws who had settled in that territory.

Having learned of that policy, which had not been kept a secret, Andy Glover might have decided that Indian Nations no longer afforded a safe refuge. Yet, on the face of it, neither did the route he and his men had been following for the past three days.

During the gang's flight from Wichita Falls, the Kid had shot and wounded one of them. Questioned about his companions' destination, the dying outlaw had replied to the effect that they were going to hell in the Palo Duro. He had died before he could clarify the statement. At first, the

1

sheriff of Wichita County had regarded the words as a lie designed to send his posse off in the wrong direction, or the deranged utterings of a man in mortal pain. All the evidence now pointed to Billy Robinson having told the truth.

There had been some debate on the first afternoon of the hunt about whether the posse should make camp on the gang's trail at sun-down, or head for the Red River and search out Glover's crossing point in the morning. Accepting the Ysabel Kid's suggestion, Laurie had decided to make camp. It had proved to be the correct decision.

Soon after moving off the next morning, the posse had found that the gang's tracks veered sharply to the west. Using the old cavalry technique of riding for an hour at a fast trot, then halting, removing the saddles and allowing the horses to roll, graze and relax for fifteen minutes, they were able to make better time than the outlaws. Slowly, but surely, they were closing the distance between them and the Glover gang.

Continuing the process of riding and halting until some of the horses were too tired to roll, the posse had reached the Pease River about twenty miles above its junction with the Red by nightfall. They had been in the vicinity of the Box V ranch house and Laurie had sent men in search of information and fresh horses to keep up their rapid pace.

The gang had swung well clear of the ranch, but returned to the river and kept going upstream. On reaching the point where the North Pease – as it had become – swung sharply to the south-west, the gang had gone north.

Making good time, the posse had tracked their quarry across what would one day become Hall and Briscoe Counties to the Red River's Prairie Dog Town Fork. On crossing over, they had discovered that the gang had once more headed west. That appeared to rule out the possibility of Glover returning to the Indian Nations after having laid a long, false trail. It could also mean that he had selected his route in the hope of bluffing the posse into turning back.

On coming to the junction of the Swisher Creek and the Prairie Dog Town Fork, Laurie had once more sought information and fresh mounts. Each had been found at Dan Torrant's Lazy T ranch. According to Torrant, there had been no sign of the outlaws near his house. However, one of his men had claimed to have seen signal smoke to the west. Torrant was of the opinion that the gang would turn back once they had become aware of it.

Sheriff Laurie had faced a difficult decision. Although he wanted to take back the gang and its loot, he felt himself responsible for the lives of his posse. In addition to the Ysabel Kid and Waco, he had along his brash, hot-headed young deputy, Eric Narrow, and four citizens. Skilled fighting men, the latter quartet each had a family in Wichita Falls. So Laurie had wondered if he was justified in taking them into the Palo Duro country.

While the other Comanche bands had made peace a few years earlier, due in some part to the Ysabel Kid's efforts,* the *Kweharehnuh*, Antelope, band had refused to do so. Returning to the wild, virtually unexplored canyons, draws and hillocks of the Tule and Palo Duro country, they had continued to live in the traditional *Nemenuh*† manner and were known strenuously to resent trespass on their domain.

After long, deep thought, Laurie had concluded that Glover knew he was being hunted and intended to bluff them into quitting. Believing that the gang would turn away before reaching the area from which the signal smoke had been seen, he had told the Kid to keep following their tracks.

Now the sheriff wondered if he had guessed wrongly.

Instead of turning away, the gang's trail had led the posse straight towards the location of the smoke. Then the Kid had made an interesting – and puzzling – discovery. A man had met Glover's party. Telling the sheriff to let the horses rest, the Kid had back-tracked the newcomer. Returning thirty minutes later, the Kid had said the man had sent up the smoke signal from the top of a hill which offered an excellent view of the surrounding terrain. He had also claimed that the man walked like an Indian, but rode a shod horse; hinting at mixed blood. Whoever he might be, he had accompanied the gang westward after the meeting.

---

*Told in *Sidewinder*.
†*Nemenuh*: 'The People', the Comanches' name for their nation.

Much to Deputy Narrow's undisguised annoyance, Laurie had consulted the Kid on what the posse ought to do next. They had closed the distance separating them from the gang to slightly over a mile. Given reasonable luck, they would catch up and capture the outlaws during the night. Against that was the danger of coming across a *Kweharehnuh* hunting party. If it should happen, the Kid believed that he could avert trouble and might even be granted permission to keep going after the gang.

On Laurie putting the situation to the posse, they had agreed to stay with him. Apart from Narrow, they had faith in the judgment of the Ysabel Kid. Possibly the deputy shared it, but he had no intention of letting it be known. To someone who did not know the facts, that faith might have seemed strange, or even misplaced.

Around six foot in height, the Kid had a wiry frame suggestive of untiring and whipcord-tough strength. Every item of his clothing, from the low-crowned, wide-brimmed J.B. Stetson hat, through bandana, vest, shirt, Levi's pants to the flat-heeled boots, was black in colour. On a gunbelt of the same sober hue, he carried a walnut-handled Dragoon Colt butt forward in a low cavalry-twist holster at the right and an ivory-hilted James Black bowie knife sheathed at the left. Across the crook of his left arm, encased in a fringed buckskin pouch of Indian manufacture, rested a Winchester Model '66 rifle.

The armament appeared out of keeping, taken with the handsome, almost babyishly-innocent aspect of his Indian-dark face. Or might if one discounted his red-hazel eyes. They implied that a savage, untrammelled wildness lay behind the black-haired Texan's youthful exterior.

Slouching apparently at ease on a horse borrowed from the Lazy T, with his magnificent white stallion – which looked as untamed as its master – loping bare-backed at his side, he exuded a sense of being more Indian than white. People who knew him were aware of how close that came to being true.

Although his mother had died giving birth to him, Loncey Dalton Ysabel had survived to be raised as a member of the *Pehnane* – Wasp, Quick-Stinger, Raider – Comanches. His maternal grandfather, Long Walker, was war chief of the Dog Soldier lodge. From that source, his father – an Irish Kentuckian called Sam Ysabel – being away much of the time on the family's business of smuggling, the child had learned all the subjects a brave-heart warrior was expected to know.*

By his fourteenth year, when he had ridden off on his first war trail, the boy had already gained the man-name *Cuchilo* by virtue of his skill in using a bowie knife. To the Mexicans along the Rio Grande, where he had helped his father on contraband-running expeditions, he became known as *Cabrito*, the Kid. The Texans with whom he had come into contact called him first Sam Ysabel's Kid, then changed it to the Ysabel Kid. Members of all three races were unanimous in their opinion that he would become a fighting man second to none and he had fulfilled the predictions. Maybe he was not *real* fast with his old Dragoon, but he could claim few peers when it came to accuracy in using a rifle.

At the outbreak of the War Between The States, the Kid and his father had joined Mosby's Raiders. The Confederate States' Government had soon found an even more useful purpose in which their specialized talents could serve the South. So they had spent the remainder of the hostilities collecting shipments of essential materials from Matamoros and delivering the goods across the Rio Grande to the authorities in Texas. Whilst doing so, the Kid had increased his reputation of being a bad man to cross.

Bushwhack lead had cut down Sam Ysabel soon after the War had ended. While searching for his father's killers, the Kid had met a man who changed the whole course of his life. The Rio Hondo gun wizard, Dusty Fog, had been conducting a mission on which the peace between the United States and Mexico hung balanced and the Kid had helped him bring it to a successful conclusion.† At the same time, the Kid had also avenged his father's murder.

* Told in *Comanche*.
† Told in *The Ysabel Kid.*

That had left him with the problem of what to do next. Smuggling was unprofitable in the War-impoverished Lone Star State and, without his father along, it had no longer appealed to him. So he had accepted Dusty Fog's offer and joined the OD Connected ranch's floating outfit.

In that way, a potentially dangerous young man had been transformed into a useful member of the community. The people of Texas could be grateful that he had. His Comanche-trained skills – silent movement, locating hidden enemies and remaining concealed from keen-eyed searchers, how to follow a track or hide his own trail, exceptional ability with a variety of weapons and at horse-handling – would have made him a formidable outlaw with no exaggerated notions about the sanctity of human life. However, since joining the elite of General Ole Devil Hardin's ranch crew, he had used his talents solely for the cause of law and order.

On resuming the hunt, the Kid had told Waco to handle the tracking. Instead of studying the marks on the ground, the Kid concentrated his efforts on scouring the terrain ahead. Having seen the youngster, whose only name was Waco, read sign during the hunt, Laurie raised no objections. The sheriff knew that the Kid was acting in a correct manner and was better occupied in locating an ambush should one be attempted.

Maybe two inches taller than the Kid, Waco had a spread to his shoulders that hinted at a powerful frame fast developing to full manhood. In dress and appearance, he was a typical Texas cowhand. Blond, blue-eyed and handsome, he wore two staghorn-butted 1860 Army Colts in the carefully-designed holsters of a well-made gunbelt. He too sat a borrowed horse and led his big, powerful paint stallion. A Winchester Model of 1873 rifle dangled from his right hand.

Like the Kid, Waco had once teetered on the verge of the owlhoot trail. Where smuggling might have brought the Indian-dark young man into conflict with the law, Waco could easily have turned into a wanted, desperate killer.

Left an orphan almost from birth by a Waco Indian raid, the blond youngster had been raised as part of a

6

North Texas rancher's sizeable family. Guns had always been a part of his life and his sixteenth birthday had seen him employed by Clay Allison. In that tough wild-onion crew, noted for their boisterous ways and generally dangerous behaviour, Waco had perfected his ability to draw fast and shoot accurately. Living constantly in the company of older men, he had grown sullen, quick to temper and ever ready to take offence. It had seemed only a matter of time before he would become involved in that one shoot-out too many which would have seen him branded as a killer, with a price on his head.

Fortunately for Waco, that day did not come. From the moment that Dusty Fog had saved his life – at considerable risk to his own – the youngster had started to change for the better.* Leaving Allison, with the Washita curly-wolf's blessing, he had found himself accepted as a member of the floating outfit. From the other members, who treated him like a favourite younger brother, he had learned many useful lessons. His skill in handling revolvers had not diminished, but he now knew *when* as well as *how* to shoot.

Six miles had fallen behind the posse since the Kid had relinquished his post as tracker. Suddenly he brought his horses to a halt.

'Stay put, boy!' he ordered as Waco's head swung in his direction.

'Yo!' the youngster answered.

'Hold it back there, sheriff,' the Kid went on, looking over his shoulder. 'I'm going to make some talk to them *Kweharehnuh* bucks up ahead.'

'*Kweh*—!' Laurie began, motioning to Narrow and the townsmen to stop and advancing to join the cowhands. 'I don't see 'em!'

'They're there,' the Kid assured him. 'So stay put. No matter what happens don't start shooting and don't come after me.'

'We won't,' promised Laurie.

'That goes for you more than any of them, boy,' the Kid said, eyeing his companion coldly.

'I hear you,' Waco drawled.

* Told in *Trigger Fast*.

7

'Mind you do it then!' growled the Kid.

'You'd reckon he didn't trust me to do it,' Waco commented to the tall wiry peace officer, as the Kid transferred to the white stallion's bare back without setting foot on the ground.

'Maybe he knows you,' Laurie replied.

'I'll fix his wagon,' threatened the young blond, without denying the allegation. 'When we get down to home, I'll lay all the blame on him for us being late back.'

On their way home after a successful and profitable trail drive to Mulrooney, Kansas, the floating outfit had called at Bent's Ford in the Indian Nations. Dusty had found a telegraph message from Ole Devil awaiting his arrival, telling him to call and see the Governor of Texas at Austin. Doing so had created something of a problem. Part of the trail herd had belonged to a friend who ranched near Throckmorton and had been unable to make the drive. After some discussion, it had been decided that the Kid should deliver the friend's share of the money brought in by the cattle.

Sharing the Indian-dark cowhand's aversion to wearing formal clothes and a neck-tie – which would most likely be expected of him when visiting the Governor – Waco had volunteered to accompany the Kid. They had been in Wichita Falls during the bank robbery and offered their services to the sheriff. Before setting out with the posse, the Kid had notified Dusty of their actions by telegraph. Neither of them felt any qualms at turning aside from their duty, knowing that Dusty and Ole Devil would approve of them doing so under the circumstances.

'What's up, Ian?' Narrow demanded as he and the four townsmen gathered around the sheriff.

'The Kid's seen some *Kweharehnuh* and's going to talk to them,' Laurie replied. 'Keep your rifles on your saddles and don't nobody shoot unless I give you the word.'

A low rumbled mutter of surprise rose from the men. They all tried, without success, to locate the Indians which the Kid had claimed he was going to interview. Ahead, the range was little different to the kind of terrain through which they had travelled all day. Rolling, broken by folds,

8

mounds and draws, it hardly seemed capable of offering hiding places for a large body of men. Apart from the solitary, black-clad figure on the huge white stallion, there was no sign of human life in front of them. As usual, Narrow was inclined to scoff.

'They must be a hell of a long ways off,' the deputy declared. 'I can't see hide nor hair of them.'

'Which's likely why the sheriff had Lon and not you riding the point,' drawled Waco.

Although Narrow let out a hiss of annoyance, he made no reply. Early in the hunt, he had found out that his assumption of tough superiority did not impress Waco. So he sat back in his saddle and watched the Kid with an air of disbelief. At the moment, Narrow found himself torn between two desires. While he looked forward to a fight with the Indians, he also hoped the Kid would prove to be wrong. Then the sheriff would stop listening to the cowhand and pay more attention to his deputy's opinions.

'Reckon he's joshing us about them *Kweharehnuh*, Waco?' asked a posseman called Bretton.

'He wouldn't know how at a time like this,' the young blond replied.

With each sequence of hoof-beats in the stallion's walking gait carrying him deeper into danger, the Kid maintained his ceaseless vigilance. Detecting the whole of the Antelope party might spell the difference between life and death. So, although he slouched casually as if a part of the horse, he had never been more alert.

Give them their full due, the *Kweharehnuh* braves sure knew how to keep out of a man's sight. Like the Kid, they must have taken seriously their childhood games of *nanip'ka*, 'guess over the hill', in which the players had to hide so that the one who was 'it' could not locate them. It offered mighty good training in concealment as well as for the discovery of hidden men.

That is, all but one of them remembered the lessons of *nanip'ka*.

Flattened on a slope behind a fair-sized rock, the solitary transgressor had allowed the single eagle's feather of his

9

head-dress to rise into view. He must be a *tuivitsi** fresh
from horse-herding and on his first man's chore. Happen
he did not improve his technique, he would never make a
tehnap,† much less reach the honoured state of *tsukup*.‡
The feather's movement in the breeze had been sufficient
to attract the Kid's attention and so spoiled what would
have been an effective ambush.

The nearer the Kid rode, the more uneasy he became. So
far, he had picked out twenty braves and feared that there
might be others still hidden from him. A gentle touch on
the reins of the stallion's hackmore ended its forward
motion about sixty yards from the nearest located Indian.
That ought to leave him sufficient distance to turn and get
the hell back to the posse happen things should go wrong.

Gripping the rifle at the wrist of the butt and end of the
barrel, he elevated it above his head. That allowed the
Kweharehnuh to see the red, white and blue patterns on the
buckskin container. With such a well-planned ambush,
there must be a *tehnap* present who would be able to identify the medicine symbols. If so, they would know the container to be a Dog Soldier's medicine boot; given to each
member of that hardy, savage lodge on his initiation.

Three times the Kid raised and lowered the rifle. Then,
taking his right hand from the butt, he turned the rifle so it
pointed forward with the barrel still in his left fist. After
that, it was just a matter of waiting. He had let them see
the medicine boot and made a sign identifying himself as a
Dog Soldier who asked to make talk. That put the play into
the *Kweharehnuh*'s hands. The next move must come from
them.

It came!

Rearing to kneel on the rock, the *tuivitsi* who had
betrayed the ambush flipped the butt of his rifle to his
shoulder and pressed its trigger.

* *Tuivitsi*: an adolescent youth.
† *Tehnap*: an experienced warrior.
‡ *Tsukup*: old man.

CHAPTER TWO

YOU'RE NOT ABOUT
TO BE COMING BACK

'They're attacking him!' screeched Bretton as the young *Kweharehnuh* brave appeared and fired in the Kid's direction.

'Come on!' Narrow shouted, starting his horse moving. 'Let's go—!'

Remembering the Kid's orders and seeing that his *amigo* had not been hit, Waco jumped his horses to swing into the other men's path.

'Stay put!' the youngster snapped and the foregrip of his Winchester slapped into his left palm as he prepared to enforce the demand should it become necessary. 'Lon's all right and he's not high-tailing it back here.'

'Do like Waco says!' the sheriff commanded. 'Form a line, just in case, but hold your fire unless I tell you different.'

When the bullet flung up dirt less than a yard in front of his horse, the Kid uttered a silent prayer that the posse would not attempt to intervene. He stiffened just a trifle, alert to pivot the stallion around and go like a bat out of hell should the need become apparent. So far, only the *tuivitsi* had thrown lead. Other *Kweharehnuh* came popping out of their hiding places, many of which hardly appeared to offer enough cover to conceal a jack-rabbit. However, they made no hostile gestures.

With a sensation of relief, the Kid noticed that a few obvious *tehnap* and a war bonnet chief were present. The latter barked an order for the *tuivitsi* to refrain from further shooting. That indicated a willingness to talk. On the other hand, to add to the Kid's concern, he observed that every man – even the youngest *tuivitsi* – carried a rifle.

And not just *a* rifle!

The weapons they held were all *repeaters*!

Looking closer, the Kid saw the big side-hammers and distinctive trigger-guards of Spencer carbines. In addition to brass-framed Winchester Model of 1866 'yellow boys', there were a few all-steel Model '73's. What was more, from the raw *tuivitsi* to the war bonnet chief, each warrior had at least one belt with bullet-loaded loops on his person.

'Who are you, white man?' called the chief in the quick-tongued dialect of the *Kweharehnuh*. 'You wear the clothes of a ride-plenty, but signal that you are a *Pehnane* Dog Soldier.'

'My name is *Cuchilo*, the Knife,' replied the Kid, using the slower-spoken *Pehnane* accent fluently. 'My grand-father is Long Walker. I come to make peace talk with my *Kweharehnuh* brothers.'

'I have heard of Long Walker, and of *Cuchilo*,' the chief admitted as the Kid rode up to him. 'But it is said that you are now a white man. And all men know that Long Walker eats the beef on the reservation.'

'Long Walker has made peace with the white men, as did chiefs of other bands,' answered the Kid, watching the braves coming closer to hear what might be said. 'Just as I now live with them. But if any man doubts that I am still one of the *Nemenuh*—'

While addressing the chief, the Kid had eased the boot from his rifle and draped it across the stallion's neck. Giving no hint of what he planned to do, he let the one-piece reins fall, swung his left leg forward and up, jumping to the ground on the horse's Indian side.* As he landed, he snapped the Winchester to his shoulder. Now his left hand held the foregrip, while the right inserted its forefinger into the triggerguard and curled the other three through the ring of the lever. Almost as soon as his feet touched the ground,

---

* Unlike the white man, the Indian mounted and dismounted on the right side.

he had the sights laid. Three times in a second and a half, blurring the lever through its reloading cycle, he sent .44 calibre bullets spinning from the muzzle.

Once again Waco displayed his quick grasp of the situation. Realizing from the Kid's apparently passive acceptance that the *tuivitsi*'s shot had been no more than a test of courage, the blond cowhand had been waiting for his *amigo*'s response. Knowing him, Waco had expected the answer to the challenge to be something sudden and dramatic.

'Keep the guns down!' Waco warned, even before the Kid's Winchester had started to crack. 'He's all right.'

Shock twisted at the *tuivitsi*'s face as he realized that the black-dressed ride-plenty, cowhand, was lining a rifle at him. Before he could make a move to counter the threat, bullets started slamming between his spread-apart knees and spattering his bare legs with flying chips of rock. Letting out a startled yelp, he bounded into the air. Coming down, he slipped from his perch and landed rump-first on the ground. Although the descent and arrival proved painful, he retained his grip on the Spencer carbine. Spitting out furious words, he tried to raise it and avenge his deflated ego.

Having expected such a reaction, the Kid was already bounding forward. Giving the *tuivitsi* no opportunity to point the Spencer his way, he lashed up with his left foot and kicked it from the other's hands. In a continuation of the attack, the Kid elevated his Winchester and propelled its metal-shod butt against the side of the brave's head. Down went the *tuivitsi*, flopping limply on to his side. Without sparing his victim as much as a glance, the Kid returned and vaulted afork the stallion's seventeen hand back as if it stood no higher than a newly born foal.

Hoots of laughter burst from the stocky, thick-bodied warriors in the antelope-hide clothing. Like most Indians, the Comanches had a lively sense of humour when amongst their own kind. They had appreciated the manner in which the Kid had handled their companion. That had been the way of a *tehnap* dealing with a *tuivitsi* who had forgotten his proper station in the band's social structure.

Fast, painful and very effective.

No matter how the Kid might be dressed, the *Kweharehnuh* braves now accepted that he was a Comanche. Every action he had made since being fired at by the *tuivitsi* had been that of an experienced name-warrior.

'Well, chief,' challenged the Kid. 'Am I still *Nemenuh*?'

'You are still *Nemenuh*, *Cuchilo*,' confirmed the chief. 'I am called Kills Something.'

'The fame of *Pakawa* has reached my ears,' the Kid said conventionally, using the other's Comanche name.

'Why do you bring white men into the land of the *Kweharehnuh*, *Cuchilo*?'

That had an ominous ring to it. Normally there would have been more talk; a lengthy delivery of compliments, or an exchange of tribal gossip. So the Kid felt puzzled by its omission. Something else was wrong, too. With Glover's gang so near, the warriors must have seen them. Yet there had not been time for the *Kweharehnuh* to have killed the five men silently and then taken up their ambush positions. It seemed unlikely that *Pakawa* would permit the smaller party to pass and go for the larger.

'We are hunting for thieves,' the Kid answered frankly, knowing that stealing from one's own people rated as a serious crime amongst the Comanches. 'The men who went by here not long ago.'

'What is it you want from us?' Kills Something inquired, but his voice held no hint of making an amiable request for information.

'To go after them and take them back to their people.'

'No!'

'They are like mad wolves, *Pakawa*,' the Kid pointed out. 'As long as such live, nobody, red or white, is safe from them.'

'I must still say no,' the chief stated.

'Can I ask why?'

'It is the order of *Paruwa Semehno* and the medicine woman *Pohawe*. They say that no white men, except the chosen, may enter our land.'

'And the four white men and the half-breed are the chosen?'

'Yes. The man of no people has the medicine, so we let them pass. Tell the men with you to turn back, *Cuchilo*.'

'What if they won't do it?'

'You are a *tehnap, Cuchilo*,' Kills Something replied. 'So you will know when it is time to fight and when to ride away. There are three of us, each with a repeating rifle, for every one of you. If you come, there will be dead men in the Land of Good Hunting. I do not think they will be *Nemenuh*. And tell the one with the star to think well on what he orders. There are young braves with me who want to count coups. Let them taste blood, and they will go looking for more. If they do, many will die.'

'All this I will remember, *Pakawa*,' promised the Kid. 'May your squaws give you many children.'

With that, the Kid turned his stallion and rode towards his companions. He did not look back. To do so would be discourteous in that it would imply a lack of trust in the warriors he was leaving.

'When do we take out after 'em, Kid?' demanded Narrow, before any of the others could speak.

'I don't reckon we can,' the Kid replied flatly.

'But we're not more'n a mile behind 'em,' the deputy protested.

'And there's twenty or more *Kweharehnuh* brave-hearts less'n half a mile ahead of us,' warned the Kid.

'So?' grunted Narrow. 'They was talking peaceable enough to you.'

'Why sure,' the Kid agreed. 'Only they'll stop acting peaceable happen we try to go by 'em.'

'I'll be damned if I've rid' this far to be turned back by a handful of tail-dragging Injuns!' Narrow bellowed, still refusing to let the others get a word in. 'I say we go on and the hell with what they figure to do about it.'

'You try it, deputy,' drawled the Kid, 'and you're not about to be coming back.'

'It's as bad as that, huh Kid?' the sheriff put in, silencing his deputy with a scowl.

'It's that bad,' the Kid confirmed. 'Every one of them, down to the youngest *tuivitsi*'s toting a repeater and enough bullets to start *two* wars. And they've been told by old Chief Ten Bears 'n' their medicine woman to keep white folk out of the Palo Duro. Unless that 'breed who met Glover's with 'em.'

'We could go 'round em—' Narrow began.

'There's not even part of a hope of doing it,' the Kid declared. 'They'll have a couple of scouts trail us and, happen we're *loco* enough to try, the rest'll be on hand so fast you'll think the hawgs've jumped us.'

'Damn it all, Kid!' growled the sheriff. 'Why should they let owlhoots go through and stop us?'

'I don't know, sheriff. It's medicine business and, rightly, they don't talk about *that* even to a feller from another *Nemenuh* band.'

'So you're saying we should go back, Kid?' asked posseman Hobart.

'That's what I'd say, was I trail bossing this posse,' the Kid answered. 'If we push on and get wiped out, those young bucks'll think they've got real strong war medicine and set off to try it out. Folks'll die then. But I'll go along with whatever the sheriff says we do.'

'Couldn't we set up camp here and wait 'em out?' asked Bretton.

'Happen they got short on patience, they're more likely to jump us than head for home,' the Kid replied. 'I could maybe get through alone and talk to old *Paruwa Semehno*. Only, way *Paruwa* spoke, I reckon I'd be wasting my time. For some reason, he's shielding them owlhoots and a whole lot farther east than I'd've figured on. Fact being, I was counting on taking Glover tonight and well clear of the *Kweharehnuh*'s range. Those bucks won't let it happen.'

'So was I,' Laurie admitted.

By bringing only a small, hand-picked posse, the sheriff had hoped to catch up with the gang before they penetrated too deeply into the Palo Duro country. Faced with the present situation, he could see only one answer. To go on meant fighting, probably getting killed. Given a victory to whet their appetite, the young bucks would sweep off on a rampage of looting and slaughter.

'What'll we do, Ian?' Bretton wanted to know.

'We go back,' the sheriff replied quietly and bitterly.

Although the townsmen, the Kid and Waco nodded their agreement, Narrow registered his disapproval.

'So we're going back with our tails dragging 'tween our legs?' the deputy snarled. 'That'll look good comes next election.'

'So'd going on and stirring up an Injun war, *hombre*,' drawled Waco.

'It's easy enough for you to talk about pulling out,' Narrow answered. 'You didn't have money in our bank.'

'I did!' Poplar, the third member of the posse, injected coldly. 'Likely more than you did, Eric. But I'm still ready to go along with whatever Ian says we should do.'

'There's no way out, Kid?' Laurie asked.

'It's turn back, or go all the way and likely stay permanent. You want me to, I can maybe sneak by the *Kweharehnuh* in the dark and go after Glover. Only there'll be none of them coming back with me and, way I'll have to travel after it's done, I'll not be able to fetch back your money.'

'I want justice, not that kind of revenge,' Laurie answered. 'No. We'll all go back.'

Guiding their horses around, the dejected posse began to ride in the direction from which they had come. Without making it obvious, the Kid kept a watch to the rear. As he had expected, they were followed at a distance by two braves. After they had covered about three miles, the sheriff joined the Kid and Waco behind the party.

'You said *all* them bucks had repeaters, Kid?' Laurie asked.

'Every last blasted one.'

'That's not usual, is it?'

'It's damned *unusual*, sheriff. You'll mostly find a few repeaters in each village. But it's near on always the chiefs and name-warriors who own 'em. And bullets're mostly in short supply.'

'Then somebody must've been selling them to the *Kweharehnuh*,' Laurie said.

'What'd the *tuivitsi* have to buy them with?' countered the Kid. 'It'd take a whole heap of trade goods to buy a repeater. More than a *tuivitsi*'d be likely to own.'

'Couldn't the *tuivitsi*'ve had the rifles give' 'em?' Waco inquired. 'You told me a warrior often gives his loot away.'

'Not a repeater, especially if there's so much ammunition around for it,' corrected the Kid. 'And, happen a war party'd pulled a raid that brought in so many rifles, we'd've heard about it.'

'It could've happened a fair time back,' the sheriff pointed out.

'Not all that long,' objected the Kid. 'Some of them were toting Model 73's and they've not been around a year yet.'

'What worries me as a peace officer,' Laurie said soberly, 'is why they let a bunch of owlhoots through.'

'And me,' admitted the Kid. 'Comanches don't cotton to thieves.'

'How about when they're wide-looping hosses?' challenged Waco.

'That's not stealing, it's raiding,' the Kid explained. 'And they don't do it again' another *Nemenuh*.'

'Do you think that old Ten Bears's been paid, either with money to buy them or the rifles and ammunition, to let Glover and his men through?'

'You mean that Glover'd fixed it up, through the 'breed they met, sheriff?' Waco asked. 'It could be, Lon. If Glover was getting hard-pushed by the Rangers and figured the Nations to be unhealthy for white owlhoots, he might've decided to come this way.'

'And sent the 'breed on ahead to dicker the way by the *Kweharehnuh* for them?' asked Laurie.

'Something like that,' agreed the blond youngster.

'Would Glover've made enough money to be able to pay for that many rep—,' the Kid began, then his head swivelled around and he pointed. 'Hey. Look there!'

Following the direction indicated by the Kid, Waco and Laurie found that a cavalry patrol was coming towards them. Fanned out in line abreast, ten privates flanked a first lieutenant, sergeant and civilian scout. Unlike the posse, who had returned their rifles to the saddleboots, the soldiers carried their Springfield carbines in their hands.

'Halt!' yelled the officer, apparently addressing the posse, for his own men kept moving. 'Halt in the name of the United States Government.'

'Means us, I'd say,' drawled the Kid.

'Best do it,' Waco commented, studying the officer's nonregulation white planter's hat, shoulder-long brown hair, the buckskin jacket over an official blue shirt and Western-style gunbelt. 'He reckons he's ole Yellow Hair Custer.'

Stopping their horses, Laurie's party watched the patrol advancing in what looked suspiciously like a skirmishing line. Instead of riding straight up, the lieutenant brought his men to a halt about fifty yards away. The soldiers did not boot their carbines. Rather they shifted the weapons to a position of greater readiness which the Kid, for one, found disconcerting and annoying.

'Who are you men?' demanded the officer in a harsh, challenging tone.

'The sheriff of Wichita County and his posse,' Laurie called back, moving slowly around so that his badge of office would be visible. 'Don't you remember me, Sergeant Gamba?'

'It's him all right, sir,' declared the stocky Italian non-com.

Not until he had received the assurance did the officer show any sign of relaxing. Ordering his men to sling their carbines, he rode forward. Asking the Kid to accompany him, Laurie went to meet the patrol.

'What brings you out this way, sheriff?' asked the officer, without the formality of an introduction.

'I was after the Glover gang,' Laurie replied. 'They robbed the bank at Wichita Falls.'

'Did you catch them?'

'Nope. The *Kweharehnuh* turned us back.'

'*Kweharehnuh*!' repeated the officer eagerly. 'Did they attack you?'

'Just told us to turn back,' corrected the sheriff.

'And, of course, you obeyed,' the lieutenant said dryly.

'Seeing's how there was twenty or more of 'em, all toting Winchesters or Spencers,' the Kid put in, 'it seemed like a right smart thing to do.'

'There were only twenty of them?'

'Maybe twenty-four, or -six. I didn't stop to take no careful trail count on them, mister. 'Specially when they could right soon get more to help out should they need 'em.'

'Where do I find them?' the officer demanded and a light of battle glowed in his eyes.

'Was you *loco* enough to go looking, they're maybe four, five miles back,' the Kid replied. 'All 'cepting two scouts who're watching us talking to you.'

'I don't see any scouts,' announced the lieutenant, after taking a cursory glance at the surrounding country.

'That figures,' the Kid sniffed. 'They're not fixing to be seen.'

Although the officer, his name was Raynor, heard the words, he ignored both them and the speaker. An ardent admirer of General George Armstrong Custer and a disciple of his policy towards Indians, Raynor saw the chance of coming to the notice of his superiors. Oblivious of the fact that he commanded a mere ten men, and they barely beyond the recruit stage, he was prepared to take on whatever force the *Kweharehnuh* might have at hand. If there was honour and distinction to be gained, however, he did not intend to share it with an obscure civilian peace officer.

'Wait here for an hour, sheriff,' Raynor ordered. 'Then we'll accompany you after the outlaws.'

'But—!' Laurie gasped, realizing what the officer meant to do.

'Handling Indians comes under the jurisdiction of the United States Army,' Raynor interrupted pompously. 'And this is far beyond the boundaries of Wichita County.'

'You mean you're fixing to lock horns with them *Kweharehnuh*,' growled the Kid, 'knowing they're all toting repeaters?'

'I shall do my duty as I see it, cowboy,' Raynor replied. 'If you'll wait here, sheriff, I'll send back word when it's safe for you to join me.'

CHAPTER THREE

YOU'RE LETTING THEM GET KILLED

Riding westwards once more at a slow walk, the posse heard the crashing of many shots from where the cavalry patrol had disappeared into a valley. It could not be said that the sound came as any great surprise to Sheriff Laurie and his companions.

Stubbornly refusing to listen to the Kid's warning, and overriding the sheriff's offers of assistance, 1st Lieutenant Raynor had insisted on taking his small body of men in search of the *Kweharehnuh*. Nothing anybody had said came close to persuading him that he was acting in a foolishly dangerous manner. The two scouts had either concealed themselves exceptionally well, or withdrawn at the sight of the posse meeting the patrol. So, on his own scout failing to locate them, Raynor had made it clear that he doubted if they had ever existed.

When the Kid had tried to pass his warning to Sergeant Gamba, Raynor had flown into a rage and threatened to arrest him for trying to seduce members of the United States Army from their duty. Laurie's intervention had saved the officer from paying the penalty for such incautious, ill-advised behaviour. Unfortunately, the damage had been done. Filled with an over-inflated sense of his own importance, Raynor had taken the Kid's words as a personal affront and refused to discuss the matter further. Repeating his order for the posse to remain at that spot until his men had cleared a way through the Indians, Raynor had set off to meet his destiny.

If it had not been for the very real danger of Raynor stirring up an Indian war, Laurie might have left the officer to his fate. As things stood, the civilians knew that they must back up the military. Allowing the patrol to cover about three-quarters of a mile, the sheriff had followed with his men.

Absorbed in daydreams of the acclaim his victory over the *Kweharehnuh* would bring, Raynor had remained in ignorance of the flagrant disobedience shown by the civilians. Concentrating on the range ahead, for they had taken the Kid's warning seriously, Gamba and the scout had evidently decided that they could forget the danger of an attack from the rear. None of the other soldiers had seen sufficient service to take the precaution of maintaining an all round watch in such a situation.

'Come up careful!' snapped the Kid, making another of his spectacular changes from the borrowed horse – remounted on his return from the interview with Kills Something – to his stallion and sending it leaping forward.

Before starting to follow the soldiers, the members of the posse had drawn their rifles. Armed and ready for battle, they set off after the Kid. Their horses might still have been walking, the way the big white – unburdened by a saddle and other equipment – drew ahead of them.

Despite the urgency of the situation, the Kid did not forget his lessons in the art of making war *Nemenuh*-fashion. He scanned the rim of the valley, searching for any scouts the *Kweharehnuh* might have placed there. Not that he really expected to find them. Acting as scouts was work for the younger braves, but not at such a moment. No properly raised *Nemenuh* warrior would be willing to take such a passive role when there was honour to be won, coups available to be counted and loot for the gathering. So the whole bunch he had met earlier would be involved in the ambush.

Given just a smidgin of good Texas luck, the posse's arrival might not be detected until it was too late for the *Kweharehnuh* to deal with them.

Approaching the rim, the Kid signalled for his horse to stop. Even before its forward momentum had ceased, he quit its back and ran on. Dropping to his stomach, he wriggled to the edge of the valley and looked over. He had expected to find the patrol in difficulties; but not in that deep.

Below the Kid, the slope descended at an easy angle and was covered with a coating of rocks and bushes. It formed one side of a narrow, winding valley through which the posse had earlier followed the Glover gang. At the time, it had struck the Kid as a good place for an ambush. Studying what lay before him, he found that his judgment had been very accurate.

Raynor sprawled motionless on his back halfway across the bottom. Close by lay his scout, his skull a hideous mess where a heavy-calibre Spencer's bullet had torn through it. One private and four dead horses completed to toll taken by the *Kweharehnuh*'s opening volley.

Hunched behind a rock at the foot of the slope, his right arm dangling limp and bloody from where a .44 Winchester ball had struck it, Sergeant Gamba held a long-barrelled Peacemaker in his left hand and yelled encouragement to his remaining men. They had lost all their horses, the Kid observed, and apparently most of their ammunition. Crouching in whatever cover they could find, they still returned the hail of lead which came hurtling their way from various points on the other slope. So far, the *Kweharehnuh* remained concealed except for brief appearances to rise and throw shots at the soldiers.

Nearer rumbled the hooves of the posse's horses. The sound slammed the Kid back to reality. There was only one way in which his party could hope to save the remnants of the patrol. Done properly, it would inflict such a defeat on the *Kweharehnuh* as to chill their desire for further riding of the war trail.

Swiftly the Kid backed away from the rim and rose. Turning, he sprinted towards his companions, waving for them to halt. While uncertain of what he wanted, the sheriff was willing to back him up. Reining in his own horse, Laurie yelled for the others to stop. All but Narrow obeyed. Every bit as hot-headed and reckless as the late Lieutenant Raynor, the deputy was too excited by the prospect of a fight to take notice of what went on around him.

The Kid spat out a curse. All too well he knew the way of the Comanche braves in that kind of a fight. Only by acting as he wanted could the posse hope to be effective in their rescue bid. So he did not mean to let the deputy spoil the plan he had in mind.

Flinging himself forward, the Kid shot out his left hand to grab the reins of Narrow's horse close to the bridle's curb chain. With a jerk, he caused the animal to turn so abruptly that it nearly fell and almost unseated its rider. By dropping his rifle and clutching the horn in both hands, Narrow saved himself from being dislodged. Rage flared in his eyes as he glared down at the Kid's unsmiling, Comanche-savage face. At that moment, the Indian-dark cowhand looked anything but young and innocent.

'What the hell—?' the deputy snarled.

'Get down, *pronto*!' answered the Kid, still holding the reins. 'If you don't, I'll gut this critter and you for making me do it!' Then he swung his gaze to the other men. 'Get off them hosses and head for the rim. Be careful. Don't let the Injuns see you and don't start shooting until I give the word.'

'Do it!' Waco advised, leaping to the ground. The fact that the Kid had said 'Injuns' instead of '*Kweharehnuh*' gave the youngster some notion of how urgently and seriously he regarded the situation.

'Come on, boys!' Laurie went on and set the townsmen an example by dismounting to dart after Waco on foot.

Leaving their horses ground-hitched by the trailing reins, the four men headed towards the rim. Retaining his grip on Narrow's reins, the Kid watched them. He nodded in satisfaction when he saw that his orders were being carried out to the letter. Then he turned his eyes to meet the deputy's.

'On your feet, or not at all, *hombre*,' the Kid warned. 'And make up your mind fast.'

'All right,' Narrow answered and swung from his saddle.

While the deputy checked his rifle, the Kid joined their

companions on the rim. Still the steady rain of bullets flew from the opposite slope, being answered by an ever-decreasing response from the soldiers. So far, fortunately, the *Kweharehnuh* did not appear to have realized that a new factor had entered the game.

'No shooting!' the Kid gritted, hearing Hobart's low-spoken exclamation of anger and seeing him lining his rifle.

'You're letting them get killed!' Narrow raged, having arrived and flattened himself alongside Waco. 'And I'm damned if I'll stand by—'

'You shoot and so do I,' the blond threatened, twisting to thrust the muzzle of his rifle into the deputy's side. 'Lon knows what he's doing.'

'Get set!' ordered the Kid, moving his rifle into position and watching the way in which the *Kweharehnuh* braves exposed themselves for longer periods when rising to shoot at the soldiers. 'They'll be charging – *Now!*'

Suddenly, bringing the final word of the Kid's warning in a sharp, loud crack, stocky warriors seemed to spout from their places of concealment.

'Brave up, brothers!' roared a young *tehnap* who wore as his war-medicine a head-dress with a pair of pronghorn antelope horns large enough to turn a white trophy hunter wild with envy. 'This is a good day to die!'

With their repeaters cracking as fast as the levers could be worked – and, in the case of the Spencers, the hammers cocked manually – the warriors hurled themselves eagerly towards the soldiers.

It was an awe-inspiring sight and made more so by the ear-splitting war-whoops which burst from each brave's lips as he charged. No bunch of unblooded soldiers, especially after having been so badly mauled, could be expected to remain unaffected in the face of such an assault. Their heads having been filled with old soldiers' stories of the consequences of defeat when Indian-fighting, the remnants of the patrol showed signs of panic. Desperately Sergeant Gamba tried to rally them.

Everything seemed to be going exactly as the *Kweharehnuh* wanted.

All but for one small, yet very significant detail.

In their excitement, the Antelopes had either overlooked or discounted the posse. Even worse for them, they had forgotten the presence of the black-dressed ride-plenty who had been educated as a Comanche and won himself the man-name *Cuchilo*.

The Kid had known that, no matter how advantageous it might be, the younger braves would not content themselves with a long-distance fight against an all but beaten enemy. Coups counted by personal contact rated too highly for that. So he had been determined to keep his party's presence unsuspected until the moment when their intervention would carry the greatest weight.

'Fire!' snapped the sheriff, at last understanding why the Kid had insisted upon waiting.

Seven rifles crashed in a ragged volley, followed by the eighth as Waco swung his Winchester away from Narrow. Down went the young *tehnap*, hit by three bullets. His antelope horn medicine had proved ineffective. Death took two more of the braves at almost the same moment. A fourth screamed and crumpled forward as red hot lead drilled through his thigh; and a fifth's 'yellow boy' was sent spinning from his grasp.

'Pour it into them!' Laurie roared, his sights swinging away from the *tehnap* who had led the charge.

Even as he worked the lever of his Winchester, the Kid knew that he had not been the only one to send a bullet into the *tehnap*. Waco would have selected another warrior, knowing how the Kid's mind worked. Probably the sheriff and that loud-mouthed deputy had gone for the buck as the most profitable – or in Narrow's case, the most impressive – target. Not that the Kid devoted much attention to the matter, being more concerned with saving what was left of the patrol.

Caught in the withering blast of fire, the braves' assault wavered. Another two warriors tumbled to the ground and the rest came to an uncertain halt.

'Get at them!' bellowed the Kid, leaping to his feet.

Giving the ringing war-yell of the *Pehnane*, the dark

cowhand bounded down the incline with the agility of a bighorn ram in a hurry. He knew that the posse must press home its advantage and avoid permitting the braves to recover. There was no sign of Kills Something, or the three oldest *tehnaps*. That figured. Warriors of their standing had earned sufficient honours and would be more respected if they stayed in the background and increased the chances of the younger brave-hearts to count coup. Seeing the attack brought to a halt, they would either rush up to give their support, or remain concealed ready to cover the other braves' retreat. In either event, they would be a force to be reckoned with. So, as he ran and cut loose with his rifle, the Kid kept a careful watch for the quartet of experienced fighters.

Waco was the first to follow the Kid's lead, beating Laurie to it by a fraction of a second. Not that the four townsmen lagged behind. Thrusting themselves to their feet, they rushed after the sheriff and cowhands. Only Narrow remained on the rim. Already his Winchester had accounted for the buck with the pronghorn head-dress and, he felt sure, cut down another *Kweharehnuh*. He wanted to increase his tally and, shooting on the run being notoriously inaccurate, he doubted if he could do it by leaving his present position.

Twisting around ready to run away, a soldier saw the approaching figures. For a moment he seemed to be on the verge of raising the revolver which dangled in his right hand. Then, recognizing that help was on hand, he turned to use the weapon against the Comanches. By his actions, he spurred his companions into continuing their resistance. They resumed their firing, adding to the *Kweharehnuhs'* confusion.

An uneasy sensation of having missed something began to eat at the Kid as he passed the soldiers. Another two strides brought him almost to the foot of the slope and produced a realization of what he had missed. While Kills Something and the older *tehnaps* would have allowed their less experienced companions to carry out the ambush, they ought to be taking a hand now things had gone wrong.

So where in hell might they be?

The outcome of the affair could easily hang upon the answer to that vitally important question.

Catching a slight hint of movement from the corner of his left eye, the Kid swung his head in that direction. What he saw handed him a shock. Instead of remaining behind the men laying the ambush, at least one of the *tehnaps* had crossed the valley. Rising from behind a large rock, the brave lined his Winchester '73 at the black-dressed cause of his companions' misfortunes. Instantly, showing the superb coordination of mind and muscles developed in his formative years, the Kid hurled himself down in a rolling dive. While his speedy response saved him from the *tehnap*'s first bullet – the wind of which stirred the back of his shirt – he felt sure the next would be better aimed. So he landed expecting to feel the flat-nosed .44.40 bullet strike his body.

As he followed the Kid, Waco saw a shape rising from amongst a clump of buffalo-berry bushes to his right. Behind the blond, the sheriff found a greater need to notice the warrior. Cradled at his shoulder, the brave's rifle was pointing at Laurie's chest. Like Waco, the sheriff held his Winchester so its barrel was pointing to the left. He doubted if he could turn it quickly enough to save his life. Waco's thoughts paralleled the sheriff's, but he came up with a different answer. Instead of trying to use the rifle, the blond held its foregrip in his left hand. Leaving the wrist of the butt, his right flashed to the staghorn butt of his off-side Army Colt.

To Waco's rear, Laurie watched everything. In his time as a peace officer, he had seen a number of real fast men in action. That tall, blond youngster, in his opinion, could have matched the best. All in a single, incredibly swift motion, Waco produced and fired the revolver. Its bullet took the *tehnap* in the centre of the torso. The breast-bone cracked, mingling with his cry of pain. He staggered and disappeared as suddenly as he had come into view.

On the rim, Narrow had found the rapidly departing braves an elusive and hard-to-hit target. Six times his rifle had spoken, without the sight of an Indian falling to delight him. So he decided that he might as well join the other members of the posse. Standing up, he observed the *tehnap* rising at the Kid's left. Presented with a stationary target, Narrow hurriedly revised his plans. Taking aim as the warrior sent the shot at the Kid, Narrow fired in echo to it.

'That's another!' the deputy enthused as the *tehnap* collapsed.

Completing his roll by springing to his feet, the Kid turned to the left and wondered why he had not been shot. He saw the *tehnap* going down and commenced a silent vote of thanks to whoever had saved his life. Even as he did so, a savage war screech caused him to forget all thoughts of gratitude.

The young *tuivitsi* was not among those making good their escape. Although he had fallen, he was unharmed. Since his humiliation at the Kid's hands, he had suffered from the mockery of his companions. So he had decided to perform a deed which would retrieve his lost honour. It had been his intention to let the newcomers join the soldiers, then rise and open fire on them – without having given any thought to how he might escape after doing it.

Seeing that his humiliator led the rescuers, the *tuivitsi* had hastily revised his scheme. There would be greater honour if he killed the man who had been responsible for his shame. Looking up, he found that the *Pehnane* was facing to the left and unaware of his presence. Thrusting himself erect with a wild yell, the inexperienced *Kweharehnuh* called attention to himself.

Snapping up his rifle, Laurie took aim and fired. Four more weapons hurled lead at the *tuivitsi*. Two of the bullets missed, but any one of the others would have been fatal and he was thrown backwards by their impact.

The Kid spun around. With the *tuivitsi* and the *tehnap* no longer menacing his existence, he looked for Kills Something. Although he figured that the chief would also be on his side of the valley, the Kid was just a shade too late in locating him.

Having positioned himself closer to the rim than the two *tehnaps*, Kills Something had found himself cut off from his companions. There was, however, a way in which the loss of honour could be lessened if not entirely removed. Already Old Man and two of the *tuivitsi* had gathered and driven off the soldiers' horses. So *Pakawa* would take the mounts of the *Pehnane* and the other white men.

Approaching the top of the slope, Kills Something had seen Narrow. Unfortunately for him, the deputy had not been equally observant. Standing erect and in plain sight, thinking of the story he would be able to tell to his cronies on returning to Wichita Falls, Narrow paid the price for his carelessness. Raising his rifle, the chief laid his sights and squeezed the trigger. Puncturing Narrow's left temple, the bullet shattered through the other side of his head. He died without knowing what had hit him.

While turning in search of the chief, the Kid had cradled the butt of the old 'yellow boy' against his right shoulder. On detecting Kills Something, he made a rough alignment of the barrel rather than the sights and started shooting. Five times, as fast as he could operate the mechanism, lead spurted from the rifle's barrel. As he fired, the Kid moved the muzzle in a horizontal arc. Fast though he acted, he failed to prevent Narrow being killed. An instant before the first of the Kid's bullets struck him, the chief had made wolf-bait of the deputy. Three of the Kid's shots found their mark and Kills Something fell out of sight beyond the rim.

Lowering his rifle, the Kid snarled out a curse at Raynor's stupidity. Then he swung back to the bottom of the valley and his companions. They showed every sign of continuing to pursue the fleeing braves and he understood the danger of doing it. Chasing surprised, dismounted Comanches was one thing. Going after them once they had reached and boarded their war ponies was a horse of a very different colour.

By the time the posse reached the top of the other slope, the braves would be in what had become a Comanche's natural state; on the back of a horse. They would then be ideally suited to escape – or to launch a counter-attack. If they selected the latter course, the posse might find them a vastly different and more dangerous proposition.

'Hold it, sheriff!' the Kid yelled. 'Let them go!'

Having reached much the same conclusions, Laurie needed only to hear the Kid's words to respond. Nor did any of the other members of the posse raise objections when Laurie called for them to stop.

'Looks like we can get after Glover's bunch again, Ian,' Poplar suggested as the men gathered about the sheriff.

'Like hell we can,' answered the Kid. 'This neck of the woods'll be all aswarm with *Kweharehnuh* once word of the fight gets around. And that'll not be long. We're going to need luck to hit Torrant's afore they jump us, with all the wounded soldiers along. The sooner we get headed that way, the better our chances of doing it.'

CHAPTER FOUR

THERE'LL BE A PRICE ON YOUR HEADS

'We got back to Torrant's without any more trouble from the *Kweharehnuh*, borrowed some hosses from him and got the wounded to Wichita Falls,' the Ysabel Kid concluded, after describing the hunt for the Glover gang and its consequences. 'Found your telegraph message waiting for us, Dusty, and come down here as fast as we could make it.'

Dirty, unshaven, showing signs of having travelled hard and at speed over a long distance, the Kid and Waco sat at the dining-room table in the log cabin maintained as a base for hunting by the Governor of Texas. Situated on the banks of the Colorado River, the building was sufficiently far from Austin to ensure Stanton Howard's privacy, yet close enough for him to be reached in an emergency.

Three more men shared the table. Big, handsome, impressive even in his hunting clothes, Governor Howard sat drumming his fingers on the wood. To his right, tall and slim in his undress uniform, Colonel Edge of the U.S. Army's Adjutant General's Department frowned at the roof. However, the Kid and Waco gave most of their attention to the third of their audience. He was the segundo of their ranch, a man for whom either of them would have given his life without hesitation. His name, Dusty Fog.

Ask almost anybody in Texas about Dusty Fog and they would have plenty to tell. How, at seventeen, he had commanded Company 'C' of the Texas Light Cavalry and earned a reputation as a military raider equal to that of

John Singleton Mosby and Turner Ashby. In addition to harassing the Yankee forces in Arkansas,* he had prevented a plot by Union fanatics to start an Indian uprising which would have decimated the Lone Star State.† It was whispered that he had assisted Belle Boyd,‡ the Rebel Spy, on two successful missions.§

With the War over and Ole Devil Hardin crippled in a riding accident,¶ Dusty had handled much business on his behalf. He had become known as a cowhand of considerable ability, trail boss equal to the best and the man who had brought law and order to two wild, wide open towns.‖ He was said to be the fastest and most accurate revolver-toter in Texas. According to all reports, he topped off his talents by being exceptionally capable at defending himself with his bare hands.

By popular conception, such a man ought to be a veritable giant in stature and handsome to boot.

Dustine Edward Marsden Fog stood no more than five foot six in his high heeled, fancy-stitched boots. Small, insignificant almost, the dusty blond Texan might appear, but he possessed a muscular development that went beyond his inches. There was a strength of will about his good-looking face and a glint in his grey eyes which hinted that he was no man to trifle with. Although his range clothing had cost good money, he gave it an air of being somebody's castoffs.

Studying Dusty, the Kid and Waco felt puzzled. Like them, he was unshaven and untidy. Nobody expected members of a hunting party to dress as neatly as if they were going to a Sunday afternoon prayer-meeting, but Dusty's appearance went beyond the usual bounds. Taken

* Told in *Kill Dusty Fog!* and *Under the Stars and Bars.*

† Told in *The Devil Gun.*

‡ Some of Belle Boyd's history is told in: *The Bloody Border, Back to the Bloody Border, The Bad Bunch* and *The Hooded Riders.*

§ Told in: *The Colt and the Sabre* and *The Rebel Spy.*

¶ Told in the 'The Paint' episode of *The Fastest Gun in Texas.*

‖ Told in: *Quiet Town, The Making of a Lawman, The Trouble Busters.*

with the pair having seen their work mounts* in the coral, guarded by the OD Connected's wrangler, Dusty's appearance suggested that something unusual was in the air.

'Why didn't the *Kweharehnuh* come after you?' asked Colonel Edge.

'We'd dropped their war bonnet chief and spoiled their medicine,' the Kid explained. 'A scout trailed us to Torrant's, watched us pull out again and turned back.'

'We wasn't a lil bit sorry to see him go,' Waco drawled.

'They wouldn't let you go after Glover's gang then?' Dusty asked.

'Nope,' confirmed the Kid. 'I'm damned if I can figure out why not. 'Less that 'breed had bought a way through for 'em by handing out repeaters.'

'You say that they *all* had repeaters, Lon?' Howard inquired.

'Every last son-of-a-bitching one, Governor,' replied the Kid. 'And plenty of shells to use in 'em.'

'Then it's true, Dusty!' Howard ejaculated.

'It's starting to look that way, sir,' the small Texan agreed. 'We know now what the *Kweharehnuh*'s price was for their part in it. A repeater and ammunition for every man'd go a long way to making them act friendly to the right sort of folk.'

'What's it all about, Dusty?' Waco asked.

'There may be a town in the Palo Duro where men on the dodge can go and hide out safe from the law,' Dusty answered.

'Hey, Lon!' Waco said. 'Maybe that's what the feller you shot meant when he said the gang was going to hell in the Palo Duro.'

'According to Jules Murat,' Dusty put in, 'that's the name of the town.'

'What?' asked Waco.

'Hell,' Dusty elaborated. 'Jules says that the town's called "Hell".'

With his two *amigos* listening and taking in every word,

---

* A Texan used the word 'mount' and not 'string' for his work horses.

Dusty went on with the explanation. Captain Jules Murat of the Texas Rangers had been trying to locate the notorious Siddons gang, without any success. Then an informer had claimed that they had gone to a town called Hell in the Palo Duro. At first Murat had been inclined to scoff at the idea. Not for long. Checking with the heads of other Ranger Companies, he had learned that several badly wanted gangs had formed the habit of disappearing as if the ground had swallowed them when things grew too hot. So he had done some more investigating and believed that the town did exist.

'From what I saw of the *Kweharehnuh* at the Fort Sorrel peace meeting, I'd've said it wasn't possible,' Dusty finished. 'Only what you'd told us is making me change my mind.'

'Jules isn't an alarmist,' Howard continued soberly. 'Such a place would be a blessing for outlaws. If I discarded the idea, it was only because I couldn't see how they could reach it in the heart of the Antelope's country.'

'You've given us the answer,' Dusty told his friends. 'According to Jules' informers, the folk who run Hell have done a deal with the *Kweharehnuh*. On top of that, they put out scouts to watch for white folks coming. Said scouts check on who they are and, if they're all right, take them past the Antelopes.'

'What's your opinion, Kid?' Edge wanted to know.

'It's possible,' the Kid admitted. 'We saw the repeaters and shells that bunch was toting. 'n' Kills Something allowed he'd had orders from old Ten Bears to keep most white folk out.'

'That 'breed was a scout for the town,' Waco declared. 'He saw Glover's bunch coming and sent up the smoke. Anybody's didn't know about it would steer clear of smoke signals. When they headed towards 'em, he knowed they was on the dodge.' He nodded. 'I like that better'n Glover having sent the 'breed on ahead with either the repeaters or the money to buy 'em. Even if Glover could trust the feller that much, it'd've cost him one hell of a pile of money.'

'Between thirty and sixty dollars apiece, depending on

which kind of rifle they handed out,' Dusty agreed. 'One gang couldn't afford an outlay like that, but a town drawing money from a lot of outlaws could.'

'Thing I don't see is how these folks at the town got friendly enough with Ten Bears to make the deal,' drawled the Kid. 'He's always been one for counting coup on the white brother first and talking a long second.'

'You're saying they couldn't have done it?' Edge queried.

'Not after what I saw out there,' corrected the Kid. 'I'm only wondering how it was done.'

'The U.S. Army's thinking of going to learn the answer to that,' Edge remarked, watching the Kid as he spoke.

'Happen you try, Colonel,' drawled the dark-faced cowhand, 'the *Kweharehnuh*'ll make whoever goes wish they hadn't.'

'The column would be adequately supported,' Edge pointed out. 'I think the Indians would find cannon and Gatling guns a match for their repeaters.'

'You don't reckon they'd be *loco* enough to lock horns with your column head on, now do you, Colonel?' the Kid countered. 'Those fellers'll be crossing Ten Bears' home range, which he knows like they'll not get the chance to learn. Maybe you'd get the *Kweharehnuh* in the end, but it'd cost you plenty of lives. And that's not counting how the news'd go with the folks on the reservations.'

'How do you mean?' Edge wanted to know.

'You take after the *Kweharehnuh* 'n' get licked, which could happen with them toting repeaters, and every bad-hat or restless buck on the reservation'll be headed for the Palo Duro to take cards. Them folks might even hand out guns to 'em to hold the Army out of the town. That happens, and we might's well never had the peace talks at Fort Sorrel. Because, Colonel, you're likely to get the whole blasted Comanche Nation cutting in.'

Going by the glance Howard darted at Edge, the Kid had been confirming points already made. For his part, the officer was surprised to hear such logic from one so young. Edge decided that the stories of the Ysabel Kid's Indian-savvy he had heard might be true. Certainly the Kid had

just expressed the arguments set out by several experienced
Indian-fighters who had been consulted by the Governor.

'What's the answer, would you say, Lon?' Howard
inquired.

'Send somebody in to see if the town's there and find out
just how far they could go to support the *Kweharehnuh*,'
the Kid answered without hesitation.

'When would be the best time to move against the
Kweharehnuh, discounting the town and its supply of
weapons?'

'Middle of autumn, Colonel. When the braves're back
from the winter-food gathering and've started to make
medicine. Send in good men then, and you might get the
band without too much fighting. I figure you've got to
fetch them in. 's long's they're out, it'll always tempt
bucks on the reservations to go and join them.'

'That's how the Army sees it, Kid,' Edge admitted. 'So
we want to know in time to get things set up ready.'

'Whoever you send in there's not going to have an easy
time,' Waco commented. 'If it's a peace officer, he's likely
to get recognized. There's maybe owlhoots from all over
Texas there.'

'That's why I won't let Jules or the other Ranger cap-
tains send in their men,' Howard said grimly. 'I don't have
to explain. We can all remember what happened in
Prairie Dog.'

For a moment, Dusty's face clouded at the painful
memory produced by the Governor's words. Sent to investigate complaints from the citizens of the town that had
been called Prairie Dog – but now bore another, less com-
plimentary name – his younger brother, Danny, had been
exposed as a member of the Texas Rangers and murdered.*

'We could go,' Waco offered eagerly. 'Ain't none of
us's held a law badge in Texas. Faking up reward posters'd
be easy enough done.'

'*Too* easy, boy,' Dusty drawled. 'It'd take a whole heap
more than just sticking made-up names on wanted dodgers

* Told in *A Town Called Yellowdog*.

to get us accepted. Whoever's running the town's no fool.
And I don't reckon he's a soft-shell do-gooder trying to
prove that all every owlhoot's needing is a second chance
to turn him into a honest man. Which means him, and the
folks in it with him, are doing it for money. Jules's heard
they take a cut of the loot from everybody who arrives.'

'So we're not going?' said the Kid, sounding disappointed.

'*We*'re not,' Dusty answered and stood up. Crossing to
the side-piece, he returned and laid a copy of the *Texas
State Gazette* on the table before the cowhands. Tapping
an item with his forefinger, he went on, 'These *hombres*
are.'

Looking down, the Kid and Waco read the article indicated by Dusty.

'U.S. ARMY PAYMASTER ROBBED
$100,000.00 *HAUL FOR GANG*

*Two weeks ago, three men robbed U.S. Army
Paymaster, Colonel Stafford J. Klegg, of one hundred
thousand dollars in bills and gold. The money, payment
for remounts and the Fort Sorrel garrison, was taken
following an ambush in which Colonel Klegg, Sergeant
Magoon and the six man escort had been shot and killed.*

*Questioned by our correspondent regarding the small
size of the escort, Colonel Edge of the Adjutant General's
Department replied, "The delivery had been kept a secret,
even from the escort. It was decided that sending more men
might arouse unwanted suspicions. Other deliveries have
been made in the same manner. All the escort were
veterans with considerable line service."*

*Colonel Edge also stated that news of the robbery had
not been released earlier so as to increase the chances of
apprehending the culprits.*

*Captain Jules Murat, commanding Company "G",
Texas Rangers, has been working in conjunction with the
Adjutant General's Department in the investigation.
Displaying the kind of efficiency we have come to expect
of this officer, Captain Murat has already uncovered*

details of the evil plot behind the robbery. According to a woman of ill-repute with whom he had been associating, Sergeant Magoon had discovered the true nature of his assignment and formed an alliance with the robbers. If so, it appears that he received his just deserts when his companions-in-crime double-crossed him and murdered him along with the rest of the escort.

Captain Murat says that the men concerned have been identified as:

EDWARD JASON CAXTON; in his mid-twenties, around five foot six in height, sturdily-built, blond-haired, grey-eyed, reasonably handsome, may be wearing cowhand clothes and carries matched white-handled Colt Civilian Model Peacemakers in cross-draw holsters. Is said to be exceptionally fast with them.

MATTHEW "BOY" CAXTON; half-brother to the above. Six foot two, blue-eyed, blond, well-built, not more than eighteen years of age. Wears cowhand clothes, and two staghorn handled 1860 Army Colts in tied-down holsters. Can draw and shoot very fast.

ALVIN "COMANCHE" BLOOD: six foot tall, lean, black-haired, with reddish-brown eyes, dark-faced. Wears buckskin shirt, Levi's and Comanche moccasins, is usually armed with a Colt Dragoon, in a low cavalry twist-hand draw holster and an ivory hilted bowie knife. Is very dangerous when roused.

A reward of $10,000.00 has been offered by the Army for the apprehension of each of the above-named men. Captain Murat warns that they are armed, desperate and should be approached with caution. He hopes to make an early arrest.'

'So that's how we're going to—' Waco began, having read the story.

'Try this one first,' Dusty suggested and indicated another item of news.

'PROTESTS OVER ARMY BEEF CONTRACT

Already vigorous protests are being lodged against a

contract to deliver beef to the Army and Navy in New Orleans having been awarded to General "Ole Devil" Hardin's OD Connected ranch. Captain Miffin Kennedy, Captain Dick King and Shangai Pierce each claims that his ranch would be better situated to make the deliveries.

Tempers were high at a recent meeting between Captain Dusty Fog of the OD Connected and the opposing ranchers. Governor Stanton Howard has intervened and is gathering the affected parties in San Antonio de Bexar for a conference to work out an equitable solution.

As the first consignment of cattle is required for shipment at Brownsville, Captain Fog will be sending his ranch's floating outfit to deliver it. He says his men will accompany the cattle to New Orleans in order to study the problems of delivery by sea.'

'Damn it!' Waco yelped, looking up from the newspaper. 'I thought I'd got what was happening, but now—'

'I didn't know we was dickering for a beef contract from the Army, Dusty,' the Kid remarked as the youngster's words trailed off. 'But you sure's hell don't get me going on no boat. They're trouble. It was boats that brought you blasted white folks to our country.'

'What do you reckon now, boy?' Dusty inquired, watching Waco.

'You, Lon 'n' me're them three miscreants who robbed the Paymaster and made wolf-bait out of poor ole Paddy Magoon,' Waco replied. 'It'll be Mark who goes as "Dusty Fog" to meet them riled-up ranchers in San Antone, while the rest of the floating outfit're hard to work driving cattle along to Brownsville and riding the boat some folks's so scared of to New Orleans.'

Surprise flickered on Edge's face at the rapid way in which the blond youngster had reached the correct conclusion. When the idea of sending in the floating outfit had been suggested, Dusty had wisely insisted on careful preparations and precautions. In addition to providing a covering story in the newspaper, he had thought up the scheme to divert attention from the trio of 'wanted men's' similarity to himself, the Kid and Waco. There had been numerous occasions in the past when people had mistaken Mark Counter for Dusty. The handsome blond giant looked like the kind of man people expected Dusty to be.* So, with the backing of the three 'protesting' ranchers, he would pose as Dusty in San Antonio. Clearly Waco understood all that.

'Anybody talks about the way you tote your guns, you can say you're copying Dusty Fog,' the Kid remarked. 'Folks mostly think about a rifle, not my hand-gun. But it's sure lucky we haven't given the boy his—Ow!'

A sharp kick to the Kid's shin, delivered by Dusty, prevented him from finishing his reference to a pair of staghorn handled, engraved Colt Artillery Peacemakers which the floating outfit had purchased as a birthday present for the youngster.

'What haven't you given me?' demanded Waco suspiciously.

'A rawhiding for leading Lon astray,' Dusty lied. 'What do you pair reckon to the notion of being owlhoots?'

'It could be dangerous,' warned the Governor. 'There'll be a price on your heads and it's high enough to arouse plenty of interest.'

'Damned if you look worth ten thousand simoleons, boy,' the Kid scoffed. 'Happen I shoot him, Governor, can I have the reward money in gold? I don't trust that paper stuff.'

'Now *me*,' countered the young blond. 'I never figured *you* was worth ten *cents*. It'll be a sure-enough pleasure not to have that blasted white goat of your'n tromping on my heels.'

In their work, which sometimes consisted of helping friends of Ole Devil Hardin out of difficulties, the floating outfit occasionally needed to keep secret their connection with the ranch. So each of them had one well-trained horse in his mount which did not bear the spread's brand. While the Kid's stallion carried no brand, it was such a

* Mark Counter's part in the floating outfit is recorded in their other stories.

distinguishable animal that he would be unable to use it. Having seen the OD Connected's wrangler – one of the few people who could handle the white with reasonable safety – at the corral, the youngster had deduced that the trio would be riding their unmarked animals.

'We'll need some money to tote along, Dusty,' the Kid said, acting as if Waco was beneath the dignity of a reply.

'And we'll have it,' Dusty answered. 'Near on a hundred thousand dollars, in new bills and gold shared between us.'

'That much?' Waco ejaculated.

'We're not playing for penny-ante stakes, boy,' Dusty warned. 'The town boss'll expect us to show him a fair sum. And, remember this, from the moment we leave here, we're the Caxton brothers and Alvin "Comanche" Blood. We'll have to fix up our story and all tell it the same way. A feller smart enough to organize that town'll not be easy to fool. We make mistakes and we'll be staying there permanent.'

'There's a rider coming at a fair lick, Dusty,' the Kid remarked. 'You gents expecting company?'

'Not that I know of,' Howard replied.

Ten minutes later, a tall, gangling man stood at the table. He was dressed like a cowhand and was a sergeant in Murat's Ranger Company. From all the signs, he had ridden hard and he wasted no time in getting down to business.

'Cap'n Jules figured you should know, Cap'n Dusty. Toby Siddons and all five of his gang've been brought in dead for the reward, up to Paducah, Cottle County. Sheriff up there's telegraphed and asked if he can pay on 'em.'

'Did Jules agree?' asked Howard.

'Not straight off,' Sergeant Sid Jethcup admitted. 'He thought Sheriff Butterfield's name sounded a mite familiar and checked. That's the third bunch of dead owlhoots that's been brought in to him for the bounty on 'em. So Cap'n Jules sent off word that he'd have to be sure it was the Siddons gang, seeing's how he'd got told they was down in San Luis Potosi.'

'What'd the sheriff say to that, Sid?' Dusty inquired,

guessing there must be something more for Jules Murat to send his sergeant. Going by Jethcup's attitude, it was of a sensational nature.

'Damned if Butterfield didn't wire straight back and say we could send a man along to identify them if we was so minded,' the sergeant replied. 'Allowed the bodies'd keep a while, seeing's the feller who brought them in'd had them embalmed.'

'Whee-dogie!' breathed Waco. 'It sounds like them fellers in Hell don't just take a share of the loot, they go the whole hawg, grab the lot and whatever bounty's on the owlhoot's head. I'm starting to think this chore could be a mite dangerous, Dusty.'

CHAPTER FIVE

WE'VE GOT TO GET OUT OF SIGHT

Dressed and armed as described in the *Texas State Gazette*, their faces bearing a ten days old growth of whiskers, Dusty Fog, the Ysabel Kid and Waco sat their unbranded horses – a *grulla*, a blue roan and a black and white *tobiano*, each a gelding – studying the terrain that lay beyond the distant Tierra Blanca Creek. They were selecting the places from which scouts employed by the citizens of Hell might be keeping watch.

In view of the news brought by Sergeant Jethcup, Dusty had insisted upon a slight variation to their plans. The trio had visited the town of Paducah to see what could be learned. While there, they had acted in a manner which had established their characters in the eyes of the customers of the Anvil Saloon. Then, as Dusty had arranged, they had escaped 'arrest' by Sheriff Butterfield, Jethcup and another Ranger. The latter had been sent along, ostensibly to identify the dead outlaws, but really to help establish Dusty's party and to check up on the local peace officers.

At the saloon, before being compelled to take a hurried departure, the trio had seen the burly, sombre-looking man who had brought in the embalmed bodies of the Siddons gang. They had also discovered that the sheriff kept pigeons, which had struck them as an unusual hobby unless the birds served another purpose.

Although a posse had been formed and set out from Paducah after them, it had not carried out its duties with any great show of determination. When night had fallen, in accordance with Dusty's plan for such a contingency, the Kid had contacted Jethcup secretly and been informed of the latest developments.

Doing so had not been difficult for a man trained as a *Pehnane* brave. Finding a place of concealment at sundown, the Kid had watched the posse, following the trio's tracks, halt and make camp. Later, he had moved closer on foot. When Jethcup had left the camp – under the pretence of going to answer the call of nature – the Kid had joined him. Hidden by bushes, holding their voices down to whispers, they had been able to talk unheard and unseen by the rest of the posse.

According to the sergeant, Butterfield had done all he could to delay the pursuit. Which suggested that the overweight sheriff was in cahoots with the people of Hell. Before Jethcup had gone to meet the Kid, Butterfield had been warning him that the 'Caxtons' and 'Comanche Blood' would soon be outside Cottle County and hinting that the posse had no legal right to keep after them once that happened. Jethcup had gone on to state that, going by the way they acted, the sheriff and the bounty hunter – who went by the name of Orville Hatchet – had not been fooled by hints the trio had dropped at the saloon about heading for the Rio Grande. Being satisfied as to their ultimate destination, the two men had been determined that they should escape to reach it.*

To provide the posse – and the Rangers – with an excuse to turn back, the Kid had stampeded their horses during the night. As Jethcup and his companion had been riding horses borrowed from the livery barn in Paducah, they suffered no loss through his action. Later, they could come out without the posse and 'lose' the trio's trail in a way that would arouse no suspicion.

Although the pursuit had been effectively halted, the trio

---

* That had puzzled the Kid, until Dusty had explained why the following day. If the trio had been arrested by the posse, their loot would have to be returned to the Army and the reward shared with the other men involved in their capture. By letting them get through to Hell, Butterfield and Hatchet could expect to make far more money.

had known they would face other difficulties before they reached Hell. If their suspicions should prove correct, Sheriff Butterfield would dispatch a pigeon carrying a message about them on his return to Paducah. As the bird could travel faster than their horses, the people who ran Hell would learn of their coming long before they could hope to arrive.

By riding west along the White River for two days, then swinging to the north, Dusty, the Kid and Waco hoped to slip past the watchers who would be sent to locate them and reach the town unescorted. Doing so might annoy the men behind the outlaws' town, but it would also impress them.

'What do you reckon, boy?' asked the Kid, as he completed his examination of the land ahead.

'I'd say up on that hill's looks like a gal's tit, alongside the nipple,' Waco replied. 'Or over to the east, top of that peak's stands higher than the rest of 'em. Them scouts could see a hell of a ways from either.'

'They're the most likely looking places, Brother Matt,' Dusty agreed, it having been decided that they would use their assumed names at all times to lessen the danger of a mistake. 'Let's hear from the heathen, though.'

'Can't be me he's meaning,' grunted the Kid when Waco look at him expectantly. 'I ain't no heathen, no matter what low company I keep.'

'Don't you never go taking no vote on that,' Waco warned. 'And quit hedging. If you can't see that far, come on out and say so like a man.'

'There's another hill, back of them two a couple of miles's they could be using,' the Kid said, after telling Waco what he thought of him. 'Can't say to anywhere else right now, though.'

'I'd seen it,' Waco declared. 'Didn't say nothing, 'cause I was testing you-all.'

'How much farther can we go, you reckon, without them seeing us?' Dusty wanted to know, giving Waco a glare that silenced him.

'Maybe's far as the Tierra Blanca,' estimated the Kid. 'To make sure, we'll keep off the sky-line as much's we

47

can. Once we're over, though, we'll have to do most of our travelling by night.'

'How do we find the town happen we do that, Comanch'?' Waco inquired.

'In the day, while we're hid up, we'll look for the chimney-smoke,' the Kid explained. 'What do you reckon, Ed?'

'Seems about right to me,' Dusty admitted. 'Let's get moving.'

Sundown found them on the edge of the Tierra Blanca Creek. Crossing it, they halted on the northern bank. Being in wooded country, the Kid announced that they could light a fire without the risk of its smoke or flames being seen. Doing so, they made coffee and cooked the last of the raw food they had brought with them. Then they pushed on through the darkness.

When the first grey light of dawn crept into the eastern sky-line, the Kid selected a draw in which they could camp through the hours of daylight. They tended to their horses before making a meal on some pemmican and jerked meat carried as emergency rations. As a precaution against being located and surprised, one of them kept watch while the other two relaxed and slept near the horses.

All through the day, with the help of a pair of field glasses acquired by Dusty from a Yankee officer during the War, the man on guard searched for *Kweharehnuh* warriors, the scouts put out by the people of Hell, or any hint of the town's position. Night fell without them having been disturbed, but neither had they seen anything to help guide them to their destination.

Another night's riding commenced as the sun disappeared beyond the western rims. It proved fortunate that night that Waco had accompanied the rest of the floating outfit in their campaign to prevent General Marcus and his accomplices provoking a war between the United States and Mexico.* During those wild days south of the Rio Grande, he had developed considerable skill in the art of silent horse movement. It was put to good use when the Kid, returning from scouting ahead, announced that they

* Told in *The Peacemakers.*

48

must go within half a mile of a bunch of resting *Kweharehnuh* braves. The nature of the surrounding terrain precluded their making a longer detour.

There followed a very tense fifteen minutes or so as the Kid, Waco and Dusty, moving in single file, had slipped by the sleeping warriors. They passed down-wind of the camp, to prevent the Indians' horses catching their scent and raising the alarm. Doing so meant that they had to remain constantly alert, ready to stop their own mounts smelling the *Kweharehnuhs'* animals and betraying their presence.

Walking with each foot testing the nature of the ground before coming down upon it, leading and keeping one's horse quiet, with at least twenty hostile *Kweharehnuh* brave-hearts close enough to detect any undue amount of sound, was a testing experience for the blond youngster. He felt sweat soaking the back of his shirt and wondered if his companions were experiencing similar emotions. Despite his normally exuberant nature and unquestionable courage, Waco was unable to hold down a sigh of relief when the Kid finally declared that they could mount up and ride.

Although he never mentioned the subject, Waco felt sure that he heard a matching response by Dusty to the Kid's words.

On travelled the trio, alert for any warning sounds and carrying their Winchesters ready for use. As dawn drew near, the Kid ranged ahead once more. He returned with disquieting news.

'From what I can see, there's no place around for us to hide in,' the dark-featured cowhand said grimly. 'Not close enough for us to reach afore it's full light, anyways.'

'Except—?' Dusty queried, having detected an inflexion in the other's voice that hinted at a not-too-palatable possibility.

'Except down at the bottom of a dry-wash we should hit afore it gets light enough to be seen from them high places.'

'So what's up with us using it?' demanded Waco.

'The sides're's steep as hell,' explained the Kid. 'Not

straight down, but close enough to it.'

'Let's take a look at it, Comanch',' Dusty drawled. 'We've got to get out of sight. If the feller sees us, he'll let those bucks know that we're here.'

Advancing across the gradually lightening range, the three young men came to the edge of a deep, wide drywash. One glance was all any of them needed to tell that there was no easy point of descent within visual distance. Nor did they have sufficient time to conduct an extensive search. It would only be a matter of five minutes at most before the high points came into view. When that happened, any lookout who was there would be able to see them.

'Hell's fire!' growled the Kid, pointing to the edge of the wash. 'A grizzly come along this way late on yesterday afternoon.'

While Dusty could not detect the tracks which had led the Kid to draw that conclusion, he felt certain that the other had made no mistake. Which only added to their difficulties. A thick coating of trees and bushes at the bottom of the wash would offer the trio all the shelter and concealment they required, if they could get down. Unfortunately, it would present the same qualities to any predatory, dangerous animal seeking for a place to den up.

There were, Dusty knew, few more dangerous creatures in the Lone Star State than a Texas flat-headed grizzly bear. More than that, *Ursus Texensis Texensis*, like the other sub-divisions of its species, was known to favour such locations as a resting place after a night's roaming in search of food.

Going down into the wash, if the bear should be in occupation, would almost certainly provoke an attack. Neither the Winchester Model '66 or '73, with respectively weak and inadequate twenty-eight and forty grain powder loads, rated as an ideal tool to stop a charging grizzly at close quarters.

'Well,' said Waco, having reached similar conclusions to Dusty and being aware of the need to take cover quickly. 'Ain't but the one way to find out if he's down there.' He paused briefly and raised his eyes to the sky. 'Lord, happen there's a bear down there and you can't help a miserable sinner like me, don't you go helping him.'

Before the other two could object, the youngster had guided his horse to the edge. For a moment, the *tobiano* hesitated, but Waco's capable handling had won its trust and confidence. So, in response to his signals, it went over. Thrusting out its front legs and tucking the hind limbs under its body, the gelding started to slide down the incline.

With the threat of an attack being made by a grizzly bear when he reached the bottom, Waco had not booted his rifle. Gripping it at the wrist of the butt in his right hand, he did his best to help the horse make the descent. Shoving his feet forward until they were level with the *tobiano*'s shoulders, he tilted his torso to the rear so that the small of his back rested on the bed-roll lashed to his cantle. He held out the rifle and raised his reins-filled left hand as an aid to maintaining his and the gelding's balance.

On completing the descent, amidst a swirl of dust and a miniature avalanche of dislodged rocks, Waco kicked up with his right leg. Allowing the reins to fall, he sprang clear of the gelding. Landing with his left hand closing upon the Winchester's foregrip, he started to throw the butt to his shoulder. There was a sudden rustling amongst the bushes, then a covey of prairie chickens burst out and winged hurriedly along the wash. Making an effort of will, the youngster refrained from shooting at them. He grinned sheepishly and hoped that his *amigos* had not noticed his involuntary action in aiming at the birds' position. Lowering the rifle, he turned and waved a cheery hand at them.

Knowing that the birds would not have been in the wash if a bear, or other dangerous animal was present, Dusty and the Kid made their descent. Each of them hoped that Waco had not seen him whip up his Winchester as the birds made their noisy appearance. Deciding that attack was the best form of defence, the small Texan gave the youngster no opportunity to comment if he had observed their hasty, unnecessary actions.

'Blasted young fool!' Dusty growled as he reined in his

grulla and glared at the unabashed blond. 'You could've got into a bad fix coming down thataways.'

'Which's why I did it,' Waco replied. 'You pair're getting too old 'n' stiff in the joints for fancy foot-stepping should you've got jumped.'

'Boy!' Dusty ejaculated. 'There's the blister-end of a shovel just waiting to be ridden when we get back to the OD Connected.'

'Matt Caxton's not likely to be going there,' Waco pointed out. 'Anyways, we're down here safe 'n' all our buttons fastened.'

That was the essential and vital point. They were now safely hidden from any lookouts who might have been posted. After some more good-natured abuse, which Waco regarded as being high praise and complete approval of his behaviour, the trio set about what had become their usual routine. Saddles and bridles were removed, hobbles fixed and the horses allowed to drink at the small stream that trickled along the centre of the wash. Leaving the animals to graze, Dusty, the Kid and Waco studied their surroundings.

Finding a place up which they could climb when night fell, they settled down to rest. Once again the man on guard searched for a concentration of smoke columns to guide them to the town, without doing so. That night, they passed unchallenged between the nearest pair of high points they had selected as lookout places. Dawn found them secure in the cover offered by an extensive clump of post oaks, on a slope that allowed them a good view of the land ahead, to the east or the west.

Hoping that they would locate the town that day, Waco volunteered to take the first spell on watch. He had only just reached his position when he gave a low whistle that caused the other two to join him.

'Smoke,' the youngster said laconically. 'Up on top of that knob there.'

'Just the one fire and made for signalling,' decided the Kid, studying the density of the column which rose from the most distant of the points he had picked back beyond the Tierra Blanca Creek. 'Only I can't see anybody for him to be signalling.'

'Keep watching, boy,' Dusty ordered. 'I don't reckon it's us he's seen and's sending up the smoke for. So I want to know who it is.'

Although Waco continued his vigil for two hours, constantly sweeping from east to west and back with the field glasses, he saw no reason for the smoke signal. Then, just as the Kid came to relieve him, he halted the movement of the glasses and stared hard at the knob.

'There's a feller coming down, L – Comanch'!' the blond announced.

'Try looking off to the east,' suggested the Kid and returned to wake Dusty.

'We've hit pay-dirt!' Waco enthused as his companions came up. 'There's four fellers coming to meet that *hombre* from the knob.'

Taking the glasses from the youngster, Dusty watched the meeting which took place. The lookout – assuming that was his purpose for being in the area – was a tall, lean, plainly-dressed Mexican and the others, four unshaven North Americans. Although they were a long way from the trio's hiding place, Dusty could make out a few details. Whatever the Mexican was saying apparently did not meet with the quartet's approval. After some talk and gesticulation, they yielded to his demands.

'Well what do you know about that?' Dusty breathed. 'The Mexican's making them hand over their gunbelts.'

'And rifles,' the Kid went on. 'Them folk who run Hell don't take chances. Their man pulls the owlhoots' teeth afore he takes them in.'

Having disarmed the four men, the Mexican led them off in a westerly direction. They went by the post oaks at a distance of around a mile and were clearly unaware of being observed by the three young Texans.

'That settles one thing,' Dusty stated. 'We're going to have to find the town instead of meeting one of their scouts. I'll be damned if I'll go there with my guns across another man's saddle.'

Going by their expressions, the Kid and Waco were in complete agreement with Dusty. The day before, they had discussed changing their arrangements if they did not find the town in the next twenty-four hours. Having witnessed the scene which had just taken place, they no longer intended to let themselves be seen by a scout and guided to Hell, if doing it meant being deprived of their weapons.

'We should be able to get a notion of where the town lies by watching 'em,' Waco suggested. 'It must be a fair ways off, though, if we still can't see their smoke.'

'They'd likely not want to meet the owlhoots too close to town,' the Kid pointed out. 'Give me the glasses, Dusty. I'll—'

'Try watching that you get the names right'd be a good thing,' Waco interrupted, delighted that the Kid had for once fallen into error.

'Go grab some sleep, you blasted paleface!' snorted the Kid.

'It'd be best, Brother Matt,' Dusty agreed. 'Watch 'em as far as you can, Comanch'. Only mind that there's likely to be another of the scouts on the knob.'

'I'll mind it,' promised the Kid.

Keeping the possibility of a second lookout in mind, the Kid remained in the trees as he watched the departing men. He picked out landmarks which would allow him to follow their route even in the dark. After they had disappeared, he concentrated on a fruitless search for the town's smoke.

In the middle of the afternoon, the scout returned. He was riding a different horse, which suggested that he had delivered the four men to Hell and obtained a fresh mount. It also implied that the town could not be too far away. Yet the Texans still could not detect any hint of it.

'I'm damned if I know what to make of it,' Dusty declared as they left the post oaks in the darkness. 'We'll go after those fellers as far as we can. Then we'll stop until it's light enough to let you follow their trail, Comanch'. It'll mean moving by daylight, but that's a chance we'll have to take.'

'We've not seen any sign of the *Kweharehnuh* for the last two days,' the Kid replied. 'Could be we're by them and the town's scouts. We ought to make it.'

Shortly after midnight, the Kid brought his roan to a halt and his signal caused the other two to do the same. Peering through the darkness, Dusty and Waco could see him sitting with his head cocked to one side as if he was straining his ears to catch some very faint sound.

'What's up, Comanch'?' Waco inquired, when the Kid allowed them to come to his side.

'I'm damned if this chore's not sending me into a tizz,' the Kid answered. 'I could've sworn I just heard a piano.'

'Where?' Dusty demanded.

'Down wind, some place. A long ways off.'

'Lordy lord!' Dusty groaned, slapping his thigh in exasperation. What've we been using for brains these last couple of days?'

'Huh?' grunted the Kid.

'We've not been making a fire during the day so's there'd be no smoke rising to give us away,' Dusty elaborated. 'And the folks at Hell do the same. Keep moving down into the wind, Comanch', and I'll bet you'll hear that piano again. Then we go to wherever it's being played and we'll be in Hell.'

CHAPTER SIX

I'LL START BY TAKING YOUR GUNS

'*By order of the Civic Council, the lighting of fires in the vicinity of the city limits is strictly prohibited during the hours of daylight.*

ANY PERSON FAILING TO COMPLY WITH THIS WILL BE SHOT

Signed: Simeon B. Lampart, Mayor.'

'Right friendly way to greet folks,' commented the Ysabel Kid dryly, indicating the sign. It was one of many similar warnings they had seen since their arrival at Hell.

With the Kid lounging afork the roan to his left and Waco astride the *tobiano* on his right, Dusty Fog rode at a leisurely pace along the town's main – in fact only – street towards the large, plank-built livery barn. No smoke rose from any chimney, which was not surprising if the penalty for disobeying the notices was enforced.

'Makes a feller wonder if it was worthwhile coming,' Waco went on and favoured the dark cowhand with a scowl. 'You and your blasted piano.'

'Them signs show you was right about why we didn't see the smoke during the day, Ed,' the Kid remarked, ignoring the blond. 'How do we play it now we've got here?'

'Any way the cards fall,' Dusty decided. 'And we'll start by letting them come to us.'

Finding the town had not been too difficult, although not quite so easy as Dusty had suggested the previous night. Riding into the wind, the Kid and, soon after, his companions had heard the faint jangling of a piano. There had been others sounds to tell them that people – and not

Indians – were ahead. At first the trio had been puzzled by the absence of glowing lights to go with the sounds of revelry. Passing through an area of dense woodland, they had learned the reason. Surrounded by the trees and erected in the bottom of an enormous basin-like crater, Hel¹ was effectively concealed until one was almost on top of it.

Although there had been considerable activity – in fact the place had the atmosphere of a Kansas railroad town at the height of the trail drive season – Dusty had decided that they would put off their arrival until morning. He had wanted to form a better idea of what they were riding into. It had also struck the trio as making good sense to conduct their entrance when they had rested and were fully alert.

Seen from the edge of the trees and by daylight, Hell had looked much the same as any other small cow-country town. Maybe a mite more prosperous than most, but giving no hint of its true nature and purpose. There did not appear to be a church or school. On the slope down which the Texans had made their entrance was a graveyard that seemed too large for the size of the town. To the rear of the livery barn, situated at the extreme western end of the street, four large, adobe-walled corrals held a number of horses.

While approaching, the trio had noticed that, apart from those along the street, all the town's buildings had been constructed of adobe many years before and more recently repaired. Wooden planks appeared to be *de rigueur* for the premises flanking the main thoroughfare. It offered much the usual selection of businesses and trades to be found in any town of comparable size. Two of the learned professions were represented by shingles advertising respectively a doctor and a lawyer. Noticeable omissions were the normally ubiquitous stagecoach depot, law enforcement offices, jail-house and bank.

The largest building in town – as might have been expected – with a size even exceeding that of the livery barn, was the two-storey high Honest Man Saloon. On its upper front verandah rail, it had a bullet-pocked name-board which was devoid of the usual descriptive illustration favoured by similar establishments.

Flanking the saloon, if somewhat overshadowed by it,

were the premises of Doctor Ludwig Connolly and Simeon Lampart, attorney-at-law. The latter was a good-sized, one-floor building of sturdy construction, with thick iron bars at the left front window that bore the inscription, 'MAYOR'S OFFICE'. Facing the Honest Man, almost matching it in length if not height, the undertaker's establishment must have had a sobering effect upon revellers with a price on their heads, or a hangman's rope awaiting them if they should be captured. Only a town with a high mortality rate could support such a large concern.

On reaching the double doors of the barn without being challenged, or even addressed, by such of the citizens as they had seen, the trio dismounted. Leading their horses inside, Dusty read the words, 'Ivan Basmanov, Prop.' painted above the front doors. Entering they found only four stalls empty and none of them adjacent to the others. Overhead, a hayloft stretched half-way across the stable portion of the building, being reached by a ladder in the centre of the frontal supports. The cooing of pigeons in the loft came to their ears as they continued to examine their surroundings. Two doors in each side wall gave access to an office, tack-, fodder- and storerooms. Opposite the front entrance, an equally large pair of doors were open to show two of the adobe corrals' gates.

Hinges creaked and a big, bulky man came from what appeared to be the barn's business office. Sullen-featured, with a heavy, drooping moustache, he wore a good quality grey shirt, Levi's pants and low-heeled Wellington-leg boots. Slanting down to his right thigh hung a gunbelt carrying an ivory-handled Remington 1861 Army revolver. It was the rig of a fast man with a gun. A flicker of surprise showed on his face as he looked from the newcomers to the otherwise deserted barn.

'Who brought you in?' demanded the man in a hard, guttural voice.

'Our hosses,' Dusty replied. 'So now we'd like to bed them down comfortable and let them rest.'

'But – But—!' the man spluttered.

'Are you that Ivan Basmanov prop. *hombre,* who's got his name on the wall outside?' Dusty asked.

'I am.'

'Then you're the feller's can say whether we can leave them or not.'

'I am also the head of the Civic Regulators,' Basmanov growled. 'Which of our guides brought you into town?'

Letting the reins slip from his fingers, Dusty moved away from the *grulla* and faced Basmanov. Releasing their horses, the Kid and Waco fanned out on either side of the small Texan.

'Can't rightly say any of them did, mister,' Dusty answered. 'We come in together and without help.'

'You reached here without being stopped by the *Kweharehnuh*, or seen by our lookouts?' The barn's proprietor almost yelped out the words.

'Is it supposed to be difficult?' Dusty countered and let a harder note creep into his voice. 'Can we put up our horses or not?'

For a moment Basmanov made no reply. He seemed to be weighing up his chances of taking a firm line against the trio. If so, he must have concluded that the odds were not in his favour. The three young men had positioned themselves in a manner that made it impossible for even the fastest hand with a gun to deal with them simultaneously.

Not only that, but Basmanov noticed a coolly confident attitude about the small Texan, except that Dusty no longer gave an impression of being small. There stood a *big* man and one fully competent in all matters *pistolero*; or the barn's owner missed his guess. In all probability, he would not even require the backing of his watchful, proddy-looking companions to deal with Basmanov.

'Put your horses up, if you want to,' the owner muttered, darting a glance at the hay-loft. Then he sucked in a breath as if steeling himself to continue. 'The price is ten dollars a night, or fifty the week, for a stall. It's seven or thirty if you want to put them in the corrals.'

'Each, or for the lot?' asked Waco coldly.

'Each!' Basmanov answered.

'That's sort of high, ain't it?' Waco challenged.

'This's no ordinary town, Brother Matt,' Dusty pointed out, concealing his pleasure at the way in which the youngster had made the correct response to permit his answer.

'Fellers like us have to pay high for what we'll get here.'

'That's true,' affirmed Basmanov, with an air of relief.

'We'll take a stall each for a week as starters, mister,' Dusty went on, returning to the *grulla*, opening his saddlebag and extracting payment for the three animals' accommodation.

'My men aren't around yet,' Basmanov commented, slightly louder than was necessary, as he accepted the money. 'If you don't mind making a start on your horses, I'll go and fetch them.'

'For what we're paying—!' Waco began, bristling with indignation.

'We can do the gent a lil favour,' Dusty interrupted. 'Let's make a start.'

Although he had taken no part in the conversation, the Kid had not been idle. His eyes and ears had continued to work, the latter gathering information that might prove of use later. Basmanov returned to his office and closed the door. Looking pointedly at the hay-loft, the Kid raised his right forefinger in a quick point and then vertically as if indicating the number 'one'. Nodding to show they understood, Dusty and the youngster selected stalls and led in their horses. While taking care of the animals, the trio discussed their plans for celebrating and Dusty warned the other two about taking too many drinks.

Basmanov still had not returned by the time the trio had off-saddled and attended to the feeding of their horses. While they did not mention the matter, each of them assumed that he had left through another door in his office and was reporting their arrival to the mayor. Each of them stood outside his horse's stall, waiting for it to finish eating. The sound of approaching footsteps and voices, one a woman's, reached their ears. It seemed unlikely that the proprietor's 'Regulators' would announce their coming in such a manner; but, instead of taking chances, the trio turned towards the front doors.

Accompanied by four young men, a small, petite, shapely and beautiful brunette entered. Dressed in a top hat, with a long, flowing silk securing band, riding habit and boots, she looked to be in her early twenties and seemed to enjoy being the centre of the quartet's attention. The riding gloves she wore concealed her marital status. Whatever it might be, going by her companions, she showed mighty poor judgment of character or a misplaced faith in human nature.

All the quartet dressed well, like cowhands after being paid off from a trail drive. Their guns hung in fast-draw holsters and they exhibited a kind of wolf-cautious meanness that screamed a warning to eyes which knew the West. Even more than his companions, that applied to the tallest newcomer.

The swarthily-handsome features of Ben Columbo had been displayed prominently on wanted posters outside most Texas law enforcement offices. He had committed a number of robberies, always killing his male victims and doing much worse to any woman unfortunate enough to fall into his hands.

Although Dusty could not place them, two of Columbo's companions probably had prices on their heads. He harboured no such doubts about the third. The last time they had met, Joey Pinter was a member of Smoky Hill Thompson's gang and Dusty had been the marshal of Mulrooney, Kansas. Luckily for the success of the trio's mission, rumour claimed that Pinter had branched out on his own recently. Dusty hoped it was true. He had no wish for Thompson, an old friend, to be in Hell, as that might complicate matters. Recalling how he had rough-handled Pinter at their last meeting, Dusty knew that the other would neither have forgotten nor forgiven him.

Everything depended on how effectively the beard served to disguise Dusty.

Becoming aware of the trio's presence, the new arrivals stopped talking. All of them looked hard at Dusty, Waco and the Kid. As yet, Pinter showed no hint of recognition.

'You are strangers,' the brunette challenged, her voice holding just a touch of a foreign accent that tended to enhance her obvious charms. 'Has my husband seen you?'

'Depends on which of these gents he is, ma'am,' Dusty replied.

'None of them. He is the mayor of Hell,' the woman explained. 'But, if he has not seen you, why are you wearing those guns?'

'I didn't know we was supposed to check them in, ma'am,' Dusty said, watching the quartet studying his party. 'Anyways, these gents're wearing their'n.'

'But yes,' agreed the brunette. 'My husband has given them permission to do so. It is the ruling of the Civic Council that no visitor may wear a gun without being given permission. Surely your guide explained that to you?'

'No, ma'am,' Dusty drawled, growing increasingly aware of the scrutiny to which Pinter was subjecting him. 'We didn't bother with no guide to get here. Still, if them's the rules, we'll play along. Let's go and see the mayor, Brother Matt, Comanch'.'

A sensation of cold annoyance bit at Columbo as he thought back to how he had been compelled, by the threat of lurking *Kweharehnuh* warriors, to hand over his weapons. That he had submitted to such an indignity and the small, insignificant stranger had avoided it aroused his anger. He knew how Giselle Lampart regarded such matters and suspected a threat to his position as her favourite escort.

'It's not that easy, *hombre*,' Columbo declared, stepping away from the woman. 'You don't walk around heeled until *after* Mayor Lampart says so.'

'Is that the for-real legal law?' Waco inquired, lounging with his left shoulder against the gate-post of the *tobiano*'s stall.

'It is here in Hell,' Columbo confirmed and, attracting one of his companions' attention, gave a nod which sent him moving towards the young blond.

'Are you the town's duly-sworn and appointed peace officers?' Dusty asked.

'You might say that,' answered Columbo. 'Which being so, I'll start by taking your guns.'

'Ma'am,' Dusty said, addressing the brunette but keeping his gaze on the men. 'Would you mind waiting outside?'

'But why?' smiled Giselle Lampart.

'If Columbo tries to take my guns, I'm going to stop

63

him,' Dusty explained in a matter-of-fact tone. 'And I'd hate to shed his blood before a beautiful and gracious lady.'

'Gallantly said, sir!' Giselle applauded, knowing her actions would act as a goad to Columbo.

'Just go wait by your hoss, Giselle,' Columbo ordered, cheeks turning red. 'This won't take but a minute.'

'My!' the brunette sighed. 'I feel just like a lady from the days of King Arthur, with the knights jousting for my favours.'

With that, Giselle strolled to where a dainty palomino gelding stood in a stall. Her whole attitude was one of complete unconcern and suggested that such incidents had become commonplace in her daily life. Reaching the gate, she turned to watch the men with an air of eager anticipation.

'All right, short-stuff,' Columbo snarled menacingly. 'Hand over the guns and nobody'll get hurt.'

'If you want 'em, you'll have to come and take 'em,' Dusty warned. 'Only, happen that's your notion, fill your hand before you start. Because if you try, I'll see you don't get the chance to rape another girl.'

'You've just got yourself killed, you short-growed son-of-a-bitch!' Columbo spat out and flickered a glance to his right. 'Watch the 'breed, Joey. You keep the kid out of it, Heck. Leave short-stuff to me, Topple.'

About to obey, Pinter became aware of the change which had apparently come over Dusty. In some way, the small Texan appeared to have gained size, bulk – and an identity which showed through the beard and the trail dirt.

Like most men who had locked horns with and been bested by Dusty Fog, Pinter had ceased to think of him in mere feet and inches. Instead, he regarded the small Texan as a *very* big, tough and capable fighting man. A man such like the bearded blond giant who loomed so menacingly before them.

Exactly like him, in fact!

'Watch him, Ben!' Pinter barked, commencing his draw. 'He's—!'

Due to his surprise and haste to deliver the warning, Pinter had made an unfortunate selection of words. Catching the urgency in his voice as he said, 'Watch him,' Columbo did not wait to hear the rest of the message. Already as tense as a spring under compression, Columbo needed little stimulation to trigger him into action. Even as Pinter tried to identify Dusty, Columbo's right hand started to grab for its gun's fancy pearl butt.

Since coming to Hell, Giselle Lampart had witnessed a number of gun fights and even provoked a few of them. So she considered herself to be a connoisseur of such matters. In her opinion – and it was the reason why she had shown him so much attention – Ben Columbo was the fastest man with a gun she had ever seen. It seemed most unlikely that his small adversary could hope to survive the encounter.

Crossing so fast that the eye could barely follow their movements, Dusty's hands closed on the bone handles of his Colts. Half a second later, the guns had left their holsters, been cocked, turned outwards, had the triggers depressed and roared so close together that the two detonations could not be detected as separate sounds. At almost the same instant, a .45 of an inch hole opened in the centre of Pinter's forehead and a second bullet caught Columbo in the centre of the chest.

Having come to a halt some twenty feet from Waco, Heck heard Pinter's shout and started his draw. Thrusting himself away from the gate, the young blond sent his right hand dipping to the off side Army Colt. Flowing swiftly from its contour-fitting holster, the gun lined and bellowed. Hit over the left eye, Heck went down with his weapon still not clear of the holster.

Having decided that his help would not be needed, Topple stood with his thumbs hooked into his gunbelt. At the sight of Columbo reeling backwards and Pinter's lifeless body spinning around, he snatched free his right hand with the intention of rectifying his mistake. Alert for such a possibility, Dusty also realized that the young outlaw possessed sufficient skill to pose a very real threat to his existence.

Cocking his Colts as they rose on the recoils' kick, Dusty swung their barrels to the right. Even as Topple's revolver started to lift in the small Texan's direction, two 250-grain bullets passed over it and into the outlaw's torso. Flung from his feet, Topple dropped his gun and crashed to the floor.

Although he had taken a serious wound, Columbo neither fell nor dropped his Colt. Bringing his bullet-propelled retreat to a halt, he tried to lift and aim his weapon. Almost of its own volition, Dusty's right hand Colt cocked, passed beneath his extended left arm and turned towards the vicious young killer. Again flame spurted from the muzzle and lead struck Columbo; still without knocking him down. Turning his left hand Colt and elevating it to eye level, Dusty took the split second needed for a rough alignment of the sights. He squeezed the trigger and the hammer fell. The top of Columbo's head seemed to burst open as the bullet drove up through the handsome face and out of his skull. Stumbling backwards, he struck the wall by the door and collapsed.

Once again Dusty thumb-cocked the Colts as their barrels lifted to the thrust of the recoil. Spinning to the left, he pointed his guns at the men who appeared through the door of the tack-room.

'Stay put until I know who you are and where you stand!' Dusty commanded.

'Which's my sentiments all along the trail,' Waco went on, turning right to cover another pair of townsmen who came out of Basmanov's office.

Satisfied that his *amigos* could attend to the new arrivals, the Kid let them get on with it. Twisting out his old Colt, he tilted its barrel towards the floor of the hay-loft.

'And tell that feller's was stamping around up there to come down, *pronto*,' the Kid continued. 'Else I'll send something up's'll make him wish he'd been more fairy-footed.'

'You are right, Ivan,' boomed the man who stood behind the barn's owner at the tack-room's door. Stepping by Basmanov, he walked towards Dusty. 'They *are* remarkable young men. Gentlemen, please put up your guns. I'm Mayor Lampart and I extend you a cordial welcome to the town of Hell.'

CHAPTER SEVEN

ONE TENTH OF YOUR LOOT

The mayor of Hell was a rubbery, blocky man of middle height, jovial-faced and with a pencil-line moustache over full lips. Clad in a well-cut grey Eastern suit, a diamond stick-pin glowing on his silk cravat, he exuded an air of disarming amiability like a professional politician.

At a word from Lampart, Basmanov ordered the man to come down from the hay-loft. The other new arrivals crowded forward to look at the four bodies. As a sign of his good faith, Dusty holstered his Colts.

'I'm right sorry I had to do that in front of your good lady, sir,' the small Texan stated, indicating the dead outlaws. 'Only you can't let that kind push you around.'

'I suppose not,' Lampart replied and gave his wife a glance. It was the first sign he had made of being aware of her presence. 'Giselle will survive it. Won't you, my dove?'

'I will,' agreed the brunette, displaying neither distress nor concern over having seen her four companions shot down. 'But I don't think Ben will be so lucky.'

'His death was only a matter of time,' Lampart said philosophically. 'A most unstable young man, with a number of objectionable traits, I always found him. And whom, may I ask, do I have the pleasure of addressing?'

'Didn't ole Lard-Guts Butterfield's pigeon get here to say we was coming?' Waco inquired, having holstered his Colt and strolled to Dusty's side.

'You know about *that*?' Lampart demanded and Basmanov let out a low exclamation in a barbaric-sounding foreign language.

'Brother Ed figured it out,' Waco explained, in a tone which implied that, with his 'brother' doing the figuring, it must be so. 'He allowed ole Lard-Guts'd send word's soon's he got back to Paducah and'd soaked his aching feet-bones in hot water.'

'Huh?' grunted the mayor, looking puzzled.'

'They do reckon doing it's good for aching feet-bones like he'd have,' Waco grinned.

'I – I'm afraid I don't understand,' Lampart told Dusty in his pompous East-Coast accent.

'Two Rangers tried to jump us in Paducah, but we got the drop on them,' Dusty elaborated. 'Sheriff had to get up a posse and come after us. We figured he'd take kind to having an excuse to stop afore he caught us, so Comanch' here went back the first night out and give him one.'

'How?' Giselle asked, staring at Dusty with considerable interest.

'He ran off all their hosses, ma'am,' Waco answered. 'Serves 'em right, for shame, fetching along that undertaker when they was chasing us.'

'Undertaker?' the brunette gasped, swivelling her gaze at her husband.

'If he warn't, he sure dressed like one,' Waco told her. 'Big, hungry-looking jasper. That gun he toted, though, he could maybe drum up some business if there wasn't any.'

While Dusty had said that the trio should try to impress the people of Hell by deducing Butterfield's connection with the town, he had also decided that they should pretend that they did not tie Hatchet in with it.

'You ran off Orv Hatchet's horse?' Giselle gurgled delightedly. 'Oh dear. What I would give to have seen his face.'

'You know the gent, ma'am?' Dusty asked.

'You made a shrewd assumption about the sheriff, Mr. Caxton,' Lampart interrupted, silencing his wife with a glare. 'Now, if you gentlemen will accompany me to my office, I will acquaint you with certain matters pertaining to the running of our community.'

'How about those four?' Dusty asked, nodding to the corpses.

'How about them?' Basmanov challenged.

'There's ten thousand dollars on Columbo's head,' Dusty replied. 'Pinter's worth another five and I'd say there's a reward on the other two.'

'So?' growled Basmanov.

'So it's a right pity we're out here and got no way of toting them someplace's we could turn 'em in,' Dusty drawled. 'Only they'd not keep above ground long enough in this heat.'

'That's true,' Lampart agreed. 'So we will accommodate them in our boothill. Leave these gentlemen of the Regulators to attend to that.'

'It's your town, Mr. Mayor,' Dusty answered. 'Get your gear, boys. We're ready when you are, sir.'

A small crowd had gathered at the front doors, being kept outside by the man from the hay-loft and some of the Regulators. These latter had the appearance of prosperous businessmen. All wore guns, but did not give the impression of being experts in their use.

Taking his wife's arm, Lampart glanced at the front doors and suggested that they leave by the side entrance. With their saddles and bridles slung over a shoulder and saddlebags dangling over the other arm, Dusty, the Kid and Waco accompanied the couple from the building. While leaving, Lampart acted as if he were watching for somebody. If that was so, the expected parties did not make an appearance. Looking relieved, Lampart led the way along the rear of the buildings.

As the party was passing the Honest Man Saloon, the centre of its rear doors opened. A statuesque, beautiful blonde woman stepped out to confront them. From the looks of her, she had not long been out of bed. Her face had no make-up and the hair was held back with a blue ribbon. One naked, shapely leg emerged provocatively through the front of her blue satin robe and it was open sufficiently low to suggest that it came close to being her only garment.

'Who was it, Simmy?' the blonde asked, in a relaxed, comradely manner that implied she made her living entertaining men.

'Ben Columbo, Joey Pinter, Heck Smith and Topple,' the mayor replied.

'I figured somebody'd get around to them,' the blonde said calmly, looking at Dusty. 'Did you take Columbo out?'

'He sure did, ma'am,' Waco enthused. 'Along of Pinter 'n' Topple. Getting a regular hawg that ways, Brother Ed is. Didn't leave but that Smith *hombre* to lil me.'

'If you burned down Heck Smith, you'd best watch out for his brothers. One of them's a limping, scar-faced runt,' the blonde warned. 'The other two look like Heck, only older, dirtier and meaner.'

'I'll mind it, ma'am,' Waco promised, ogling the woman's richly endowed frame with frank, juvenile admiration.

'You're new here,' the blonde hinted, ignoring the youngster and directing the words to Dusty.

'This is Edward and Matthew Caxton, and Alvin Blood, Emma,' the mayor introduced. 'Gentlemen, may I present Miss Emma Nene, the owner of the Honest Man.'

'Right pleased to know you, ma'am,' Dusty said.

'We've been expecting you,' Emma Nene declared. 'Hey! Seeing how you boys made wolf-bait of them four lameheaded yacks, the drinks are on me tonight.'

'Then we'll be in there, a-drinking free, regular 'n' plentiful, ma'am,' Waco assured her. ' 'Cause we done got every last blasted one of 'em.'

'Shall we take these gentlemen to your office, Simeon?' Giselle suggested, her voice and attitude showing that she did not like the blonde.

'Of course,' Lampart agreed. 'If you'll excuse us, Emma—?'

'Why not,' the blonde answered. 'The shooting woke me up, but I reckon I can get to sleep again. Don't you boys forget to come around tonight, mind.'

'Ma'am,' Waco declared fervently, keeping his gaze fixed on the valley between the hillocks of her breasts. 'You just couldn't keep us away.'

Walking on. Dusty was conscious of the blonde's eyes following him. The party turned along the alley separating the saloon from what was apparently the Lamparts' home as well as his place of business. The front door opened into a pleasantly-decorated hall. To the left, a sign on the door in the centre of the wall announced 'Mayor's Office' and at the right was the entrance to Lampart's second room in which, apparently, he carried out his duties as attorney-at-law. Excusing herself, with a dazzling smile at Dusty, Giselle disappeared through a curtain-draped opening leading to the rear half of the building. Lampart opened up the mayor's chambers and waved the Texans to enter.

As Dusty passed through the doorway, he noticed the thickness of the interior wall. He concluded that, if those on the outside were equally sturdy, the room would be secure from unwanted visitors. That view was increased by the stout timbers of the door and heavily barred windows. The room itself proved to be a comfortable, but functional, place of business. In its centre, a large desk faced the door. On its otherwise empty top, an ivory-handled Colt Civilian Peacemaker lay conveniently placed for the right hand of anybody who sat behind the desk. The reason for the cocked revolver and sturdy fittings might be found in the steel-bound oak boxes which formed a line along two of the walls.

While his guests were setting down their saddles and freeing the money-bags, Lampart drew three chairs to the front of the desk. He waved the trio to sit down and went to occupy the chair behind the desk, but kept his right hand well away from the revolver.

'Now, gentlemen,' Lampart said, producing a box of cigars from the right side drawer and offering it to Dusty. 'You will understand that, as mayor of this somewhat special community, I must ask questions which might sound impolite.'

'Ask ahead,' Dusty authorized, accepting a cigar. He opened the left bag and took a copy of the *Texas State Gazette* from it. 'This'll tell you the parts Sheriff Butterfield couldn't get on his message.'

While Lampart examined the paper, Dusty, the Kid and Waco lit up their cigars. After a short time, the mayor raised his eyes and nodded.

'This clears up some of the details, but there are others which require further clarification.'

'Fire them at us,' offered Dusty.

'Since bringing Hell into being, I have, naturally, gained considerable knowledge of outlaws in Texas, New Mexico and the Indian Nations. Yet I have never heard any of your names mentioned.'

'That figures, Matt, Comanch' and I've never pulled a robbery afore this one. But it was too good a chance to miss.'

'You must have been fortunate to have met this Sergeant Magoon,' Lampart remarked, tapping the paper with his forefinger.

'Not all the way,' Dusty objected. 'Sure, it was lucky meeting him at the right time. But we'd knowed him afore when we joined the Cavalry. Fact being, we'd done one of those payroll deliveries, afore they got wise to the boy's real age and talked about heaving him out. We all quit afore they could do it. Then one night we met Magoon in a saloon. He was drunk and talking mean about the Army, 'cause they'd passed him over for top-sergeant. While he was belly-aching about it, he let enough slip for me to figure he was on one of the escorts. We got him more liquor and talked him 'round to our way of thinking. After that, it was easy. We knew where, when and how to hit.'

'And Magoon?'

'Once a talker, allus a talker's how I see it. Happen we'd given him a share, he'd've got stinking drunk and bawled it to the world what he'd done. So we dropped him.'

'Only the bastard'd already done some lip-flapping,' Waco put in indignantly. 'That's how the Rangers got on to us so quick.'

'It's possible,' Lampart said non-committally. 'How did you know about Hell?'

'Man learns more than soldiering in the Army,' Dusty replied. 'Was a feller who'd been on the dodge and he told us about it. So, soon's we heard the Rangers knowed us, we came on up here.'

'But how did you avoid the Indians and our scouts, and find the town?'

'Comanch' was raised Injun,' Waco answered. 'He brought us through's easy's falling off a log.'

'Not all that easy, boy,' Dusty objected. 'Fact being, we had some luck in doing it. We travelled by night all the time until we found the tracks of shod horses. Allowed they must be coming here and followed them in.'

'What made you suspect Butterfield?' Lampart wanted to know.

'He dresses a heap too well for a John Law in a one-hoss county,' Dusty replied. 'Saw the pigeons on the way in and found out who they belonged to. The rest was easy. Somebody was paying him good, and it wasn't the citizens of Cottle County. So it near on had to be you folks in Hell, having him pass the word about anything's happened or owlhoots headed your way.'

'That's shrewd thinking,' Lampart praised.

'Are you satisfied with us now?' Dusty inquired.

'I am, although I may ask you to supply further details or to clear up a few points later.'

'That's all right with us,' Dusty declared.

'Then there is only one thing more to be settled,' Lampart announced. 'The matter of payment for the benefits we offer you.'

'How much'd that come to?' Waco asked suspiciously.

'One tenth of your loot,' Lampart said, with the air of expecting to hear protests.

'A *tenth*!' Waco yelped, acting his part with customary skill.

'That's a fair price,' Dusty drawled.

'Fair!' Waco spat back. 'Hell, Brother Ed, that's—'

'Your brother is aware of the advantages, young man,' Lampart said calmly. 'If I know the Army, much of the paper money is in new, easily-traced bills.'

'Yeah,' the youngster mumbled. 'It is!'

'So there is nowhere in Texas, or even in the whole country, where you can chance spending it for some considerable time to come,' Lampart enlarged. 'If you tried, you'd bring the law down on your heads. One tenth is a small price to pay for your safety, and that is what you get for your money. Not only safety. Here, you can find girls,

73

gambling, drinking, clothing. Everything in fact that you committed the robbery to get. And without needing to watch over your shoulder while you're enjoying them.'

'And when the money's gone?' Dusty asked.

'You will be faced with the same solution to that as would await you anywhere else,' Lampart replied. 'Work for, or steal, some more. Our guides will take you out by the *Kweharehnuh* so that you can do it. Occasionally, we are in a position to suggest further – employment – to men we can trust to come back.'

'You're saying we can stay here, whooping it up, as long's our money lasts out,' drawled the Kid. 'Then we get told to leave?'

'Of course we don't tell you to leave,' objected Lampart. 'Unfortunately, supplies cost us more than they would in an ordinary town. So the chances of obtaining charity are correspondingly smaller. And no man of spirit likes to live on hand-outs, does he?'

'Way you put it, the deal sounds reasonable to me,' commented the Kid. 'Do we go in on the pot, Ed?'

'We go in,' Dusty confirmed. 'Count out ten thousand dollars and give it to his honour, Brother Matt.'

'You say so, Brother Ed,' Waco muttered. 'Lend me a hand, Comanch'.'

'Where can we bed down, sir?' Dusty said as his companions started to count out wads of new bills.

'At the hotel,' the mayor suggested. 'You'll find it at the other end of the street to the livery barn. There's sure to be at least two empty rooms. But the prices are high—'

'Same's at the barn!' grunted Waco, stopping counting.

'And for the same reason,' Dusty pointed out. 'These folks here have a whole slew of expenses other towns don't.'

'That's true,' agreed Lampart, eyeing Dusty in a calculating manner. 'If you wish, gentlemen, you may leave the bulk of your money here. In one of those boxes, to which you alone will have the keys. You can, of course, draw it out as and when you need it.'

'That's a smart notion,' Dusty declared, silencing Waco's protest before it could be made. With the youngster scowling in a convincingly suspicious manner, he went on, 'Hold back five hundred for each of us, Comanch', and put the rest in one of the boxes.'

'You trust me?' Lampart smiled.

'Why shouldn't I?' countered Dusty. 'You don't need to bother robbing us. Sooner or later, you or one of the other folks'll get most of our money without going to that much trouble.'

'How do you mean?' Waco growled.

'Who else do we spend it with while we're here?' Dusty asked. ' 'Sides which, setting up this place cost too much and running it's too profitable for the folks to want it spoiling that way.'

'As I have said before, Mr. Caxton,' Lampart declared, 'you are a most perceptive young man. Taken with your gun-savvy, that makes a formidable combination.'

'Comes in handy to have it on your side, sir,' Dusty remarked. 'Which box do we use?'

With the payment made, the remainder of the money was placed in one of the boxes. Dusty pocketed his five hundred dollars and the keys. Going to the door, Lampart opened it and his wife entered carrying a tray.

'Mr. Caxton and his friends will be staying, my dove,' the mayor said.

'Good,' Giselle answered, pouring out cups of coffee.

While drinking and making idle conversation, they heard the front door open. Going to investigate, Lampart returned with two of the men who had been in the barn. He introduced them as Manny Goldberg, the owner of the hotel, and Jean le Blanc, the barber. Middle-sized and Gallic-looking, le Blanc started to talk.

'I have seen Pinter's gang and they are not concerned with avenging his death. Money is short with them and they are considering leaving; have been wanting to for the past few days, but he wouldn't go. Topple's leader is more relieved than angry as he was getting ambitious and, with Columbo's backing, might have taken over the gang.'

'That leaves Columbo's bunch,' Dusty drawled.

'They are the Smith brothers,' le Blanc replied. 'At the moment, all three are at Dolly's whore-house and too drunk to cause you any trouble. But you must walk warily in their presence, *mes braves*.'

'They can walk warily 'round us,' Waco snorted truculently.

'How does the town stand on it, happen we have to take their toes up, Mr. Lampart?' Dusty wanted to know.

'We let our visitors settle such matters amongst themselves,' the mayor replied. 'Beyond the city limits for preference. There's a hollow in which duels can be fought without endangering civic property or innocent by-standers.'

'Happen they want it that way, we'll go there with them,' Dusty said. 'But the first move'll come from them. You hear me, Comanch', Brother Matt?'

'I hear,' grunted the Kid.

'You, Brother Matt?' Dusty demanded, a grimmer timbre creeping into his voice.

'All right,' Waco answered in a grudgingly resigned tone. 'I hear you.'

Interested eyes studied the trio as they left the mayor's house and walked along the street to the hotel, but nobody interfered with them in any way. They had been told by Goldberg to go and ask for rooms, while le Blanc had put the facilities of his shop and bath-house at their services. Walking along the centre of the street, a logical precaution considering what had happened at the livery barn and the presence of Heck Smith's brothers in town, they were able to talk without the risk of being overheard.

'Lampart's interested in you-all, Brother Ed,' Waco drawled.

'Let's hope he stays that way,' the Kid went on, for the plan was that they should gain the confidence of the town's boss.

'Happen he does,' Dusty warned, 'you pair might have to watch how you go.'

'Why?' Waco asked.

'He could figure I'll be more use to him – and safe – with you both dead,' Dusty explained.

CHAPTER EIGHT

IT WAS ME HE WANTED SAVING

'I saw a big-pig Yankee marshal a-coming down the street,
Got two big sixguns in his hands 'n' looks fierce enough to eat.'

Sitting in a cubicle of the barber's bath-house, the Ysabel Kid raised his pleasant tenor voice in a song guaranteed to start a fight with peace officers anywhere north of the Mason-Dixon line. As he sang, he soaped his lean brown torso with lather raised on a wash-cloth and let the heat of a tub full of water soothe him after the long journey. Close by, his gunbelt lay across the seat of the chair which also held a towel and his newly-bought clothes. His old garments lay on the floor where he had dropped them as he undressed.

On their arrival at the hotel, Dusty, the Kid and Waco had been allocated quarters. Dusty would occupy a small single room and his companions share another with two double beds. The building had offered a good standard of comfort and cleanliness, which was not surprising considering that the management charged three times the normal tariff.

With their saddles and rifles locked away, the trio had set off to buy new clothes and freshen up their appearances. The bathroom section of the barber's premises had only two cubicles, so the Kid had allowed his companions to make use of them first. With Dusty and Waco finished and gone into the front half of the building, the Kid had taken his turn in a hot bath.

> *'Now big-pig Yankee stay away, stay right away from*
> *   me,*
> *I'm just one lil Texas boy 'n' scared as I can be.'*

Having rendered the chorus, the Kid prepared to give out the second verse. He heard a soft, stealthy foot-fall outside the cubicle and its door began to inch open. Even as he opened his mouth to call out that it was occupied, shots thundered from the front section of the building.

Like the hotel, the barber's shop had furnishings and fittings worthy of any city's high-rent district. It offered two comfortable, well-padded leather swivel chairs, white towels and cloths. On a shelf in front of a large mirror stood bottles of lotions, hair-tonics, patent medicines and other products of the tonsorial arts.

Lounging at ease in the right hand chair, Dusty allowed le Blanc to work on his head with combs and scissors. The barber carried out his task with a deft touch. Incompetence at his trade had not been the reason why he had settled and gone into business in Hell. Waco was in the second chair, with le Blanc's tall, lean young assistant trimming his hair.

Although Dusty was seated with his back to the door, the big mirror allowed him to keep watch on it. With the type of customer he catered for, le Blanc must have been compelled to have such a fitting installed. No man with a price on his head took to the notion of having people come up behind him, unless he had the means to keep an eye on them.

All the time the scissors were clicking, Dusty kept the door under observation. That was partly caution, but also because of the interest le Blanc and the assistant showed in what was going on outside. Ever since Dusty and Waco had taken their seats, the two barbers had repeatedly glanced through the window at the far side of the street.

'You wish the beard removed. *M'sieur* Caxton?' le Blanc inquired as he was putting the finishing touches to Dusty's hair.

'Trim it up a mite is all,' the small Texan replied. 'I've always found the gals go for a feller with hair on his face. They want to know if it tickles when he kisses them.'

'That is a very good reason,' le Blanc smiled, throwing another look at the window and stiffening slightly. He laid his left hand on the back of the chair. 'I will make it so that the ladies fall in love with you at first sight.'

At that moment, two men walked into the shop. Tall, lean, the first looked like an older, dirtier and meaner version of the late Heck Smith; he moved to his left. The other was smaller, with a long scar twisting his right cheek. As he stepped to his right, he exhibited a noticeable limp. Even without seeing their hands dropping towards holstered revolvers, Dusty had decided that they must be the dead man's brothers. Nor did it call for any deep thought to realize that they had come to take revenge for the killing of their kinsman and gang's leader.

The man who entered the Kid's cubicle had a sufficiently strong family resemblance to Heck Smith for there to be no need to swap introductions. Tall, young, hard-eyed, he was already drawing his Army Colt. Glancing first at the dirty buckskins on the floor, he swivelled his eyes to the figure in the bath. Indignant at the invasion of his privacy, the Kid knew who the man must be and why he had come. Things looked desperate for the Indian-dark cowhand, but that brief interval while the intruder checked his identity gave him all the respite he needed.

Before the man could slant the revolver his way, the Kid acted with typical *Pehnane* speed. Swinging up the soapy wash-cloth, he flung it so that it hit and wrapped wetly around Smith's face. Letting out a startled, muffled yelp, the man grabbed at the cloth with his empty left hand in an attempt to restore his obliterated vision.

Bringing down the hand that had flung the cloth, the Kid used it to help him rise and drop over the edge of the bath. Landing on the floor, he rolled across his old clothes to the chair. Gripping the front leg with his left hand to hold the chair steady, he folded the fingers of his right fist about the ivory hilt of the bowie knife. Looking over his shoulder, he took aim and plucked the great knife from its sheath. Then

79

he swung his right arm parallel to the floor, releasing his hold on the weapon at the appropriate moment.

The knife hissed through the air as the would-be killer tore the soaking cloth from his features. Vision returned too late to save him. Flying on a horizontal plane, the clip point spiked between two of his ribs. The weight, balance and design of the weapon – brought to perfection at the instigation of a master knife-fighter – caused it to drive on until it impaled his heart. Letting his gun fall, he clutched ineffectively at where the hilt rose from his torso. Then he stumbled and blundered helplessly out of the cubicle.

Coming to his feet, as naked as the day he was born, the Kid jerked the Dragoon Colt from its holster. Cocking it, he made for the door. He heard voices from the front of the building. Realizing that he could not go there in his current state of undress, he returned and draped a towel about his waist.

Bad though the position might appear, Dusty knew that it was not entirely hopeless for Waco or himself. Their gunbelts were hanging with their hats on the sets of wapiti horns fixed to the wall for that purpose. If the Smith brothers had been more observant, they might have noticed that both the belts had something missing. Each of their prospective victims, did the brothers but know it, was nursing his right hand Colt under the long cloth which the barber had draped around his neck to protect his new clothing. All that remained for the OD Connected men to do was spring from the chairs, turn and face their respective assailants – if they could do it before the outlaws' guns came out and threw lead into them.

About to shove himself from his seat, Dusty felt it starting to move. Gripping the back of the chair, le Blanc tugged sharply at it. Instead of trying to jump, Dusty gambled on a hunch and allowed himself to be carried around. Sure enough, the barber halted the chair as its occupant faced Smith.

Shock twisted briefly at the tall outlaw's face as he took in the sight. He opened his mouth to speak. Then the cloth covering Dusty from the neck down formed a pyramid. Flame burst from its apex and a bullet twirled across the room into the man's head. All expression left his face and his mouth dangled open without words leaving it. Reeling backwards, he collided with the wall and slid down it until he sat in a heap on the floor.

If anything, Waco had been slightly better prepared than Dusty for the pair's arrival. From his seat, he had been able to see the door and out of the left-hand window. With his attention drawn that way by the assistant barber's behaviour, he had observed two men crossing the street at an angle that would bring them to the door of the shop. At least, he had assumed that to be their destination when he had noticed the taller's resemblance to Heck Smith and the other's scarred face.

There had not been time for Waco to warn Dusty of the danger. However, the youngster assumed that his 'brother' was equally alert to its possibility. So, like Dusty, Waco was preparing to leap from his seat when the assistant barber started to swing it around.

Seeing that le Blanc had treated Dusty the same way, Waco formed rapid conclusions from the actions of the barbers. It seemed that the two townsmen intended to help their customers escape from the gun-trap. Yet in his eagerness to do so, the assistant had put too much force into his pull on the back of Waco's chair. The youngster knew that it was turning too fast to halt when he faced Heck Smith's limping brother.

With Waco, to think was to act. Ramming his shoulders against the back of the chair, he used them to thrust himself sideways and roll off it. The smallest Smith proved to be faster than any of his brothers. Out flashed his revolver and lined at the blond cowhand's chair. Smith was still trying to correct his aim in the light of Waco's actions when the gun crashed. Lead winged above Waco and embedded itself in the back of the seat he had just deserted.

Tearing off the barber's cloth as he fell, Waco landed on his left side and continued to roll. As his back came to rest on the floor, he stabbed forward the long-barrelled Army Colt. Already cocked, it roared and missed. Across lashed his left hand, its heel catching the spur of the Colt's hammer and carrying the mechanism to fully cocked, while his forefinger held back the trigger. On being released, the hammer flew forward and set off another load. Three times Waco repeated the process.

Fanning the hammer offered the fastest known method of emptying the cylinder of a single-action revolver, but had never been noted for accuracy. During the one and a half seconds taken by Waco to get off the shots, the method proved accurate enough. Although scattered about his body, all four bullets struck Smith. Dropping his smoking gun, so that it fired and sent a bullet into the floor, he pitched headlong across the room and crumpled lifeless in a corner.

Snatching off the smouldering white cloth, which had been ignited by the Peacemaker's muzzle-blast, Dusty tossed it aside and stepped from the chair. While treading on it to put out the fire, he looked to where Waco was rising, 'Are you all right, boy?' Dusty asked.

'He missed,' the youngster replied. 'Hey! There's three of 'em. Maybe the other's gone—'

'Hell, yes!' Dusty spat out and darted to the door which gave access to the bathroom.

Going through, with Waco on his heels, Dusty almost tripped over the body of the Kid's victim. Dragoon in hand, the Indian-dark cowhand stepped cautiously out of the cubicle. The weapon lined at them, then lowered.

'Figured you'd be all right,' the Kid remarked calmly. 'Only I didn't aim to take no chances was I wrong.'

'Damned if he ain't gone back to the war-whoops, Brother Ed,' Waco grinned, eyeing the towel which formed the Kid's only item of clothing. 'That sure is one fancy lil breech cloth.'

'He'll send all them sweet lil *naivis** into a tizz happen he wears it at a Give-Away dance,' Dusty agreed, watching the Kid retrieve his bowie knife.

'I *allus* did,' declared the Kid and stalked with what dignity he could muster into the cubicle. 'Why'n't you blasted palefaces go leave a man to take his bath in peace?'

Returning to the barber's shop portion of the building,

---

* *Naivi:* an adolescent Comanche girl.

the Texans found le Blanc and his assistant examining the bodies.

'They cashed in?' Dusty inquired.

'I've never seen anybody more cashed in,' le Blanc answered cheerfully.

'Toby Siddons ought to be grateful to you, Mr. Caxton,' the assistant went on, looking at Waco in a worried manner. 'Limpy Smith shot him in the back two weeks ago.'

'It's nice to know we've shot somebody and won't have another bunch coming after us,' Waco replied. 'Wonder if Toby'll set up the drinks for us, Brother Ed?'

'It's not likely,' the assistant warned. 'Toby's dead and buried in our boothill. His gang left just after the funeral to see if they could raise some more money.'

From the way in which he spoke, the assistant was acting like a man trying to stop another thinking about a mistake he had recently made. Despite having certain suspicions, Waco wanted to convince le Blanc that he suspected nothing about having been treated in a different manner to Dusty.

'Anyways, *gracias, amigo,*' the youngster said to the assistant. 'You sure saved my hide. Only, should it happen again, don't shove the chair so hard. You near on spun me all the way 'round instead of towards him.'

'I – I'm sorry,' the assistant said, exhibiting signs of alarm.

'Shuckens. You've got no call to be, seeing's you saved my life,' Waco assured him. 'Likely you was's surprised's Brother Ed 'n' me when they come busting in. But you acted for the best and I'm right grateful.'

Several people, including Lampart and Basmanov, had heard the shooting and come to investigate. As at the livery barn, a couple of townsmen stood at the door and kept the curious onlookers outside the shop.

'There's another of them,' the mayor announced, glancing at the bodies. 'He might have gone after Mr. Blood.'

'He did,' Waco admitted. 'Had he asked, I could've told him not to. Ole Comanch's a mite touchy who he shares his bath with.'

'Mr. Blood isn't injured?' Lampart inquired.

'Nope,' grinned Waco. 'But he's sure a sight to see, with that lil ole towel wrapped around him.'

While the mayor was talking with Waco, Dusty watched Basmanov examine the two corpses. To the small Texan, it seemed that the owner of the livery barn looked a mite relieved at discovering that both had been killed almost instantaneously and so would have been unable to do any talking before they died.

'I never thought they'd come after you so soon, Mr. Caxton,' Lampart remarked to Dusty.

'Or me,' growled Waco. 'After we was told about them being stinking drunk.'

'Easy, boy,' Dusty ordered. 'They must've got sobered up when they heard what had happened—'

'They didn't hear about it from Manny and me!' le Blanc declared.

'If they had, you wouldn't't've saved us the way you did, sir,' Dusty replied soothingly and saw Basmanov dart a scowling glance at the barber. 'Or they maybe wasn't's drunk as they made out. Would there be anybody else likely to take this up for them, Mr. Lampart?'

'I shouldn't think so,' the mayor answered. 'They weren't the most popular or likeable of our visitors. And, in view of what's happened since you came, there'll be second thoughts before *anybody* decides to go up against you gentlemen. By the way, Ed – if I may dispense with formality—?'

'Feel free, sir. It's your town.'

'It's remiss of me not to have done so earlier, but my wife and I are giving a dinner-party for the gang leaders tonight at the hotel and we would like to offer you an invitation to attend.'

'Just me?'

'Meaning no disrespect to your brother and Mr. Blood, it is only for the gang's *leaders*,' Lampart apologized. 'Much as I would enjoy your company, gentlemen, I can't invite you without asking along all the other visitors.'

'Well,' Dusty began hesitantly. 'That being the case, I don't—'

'Aw. You go on and go to it, Brother Ed,' Waco suggested, his attitude hinting that he would not be averse to being away from his 'elder brother' with a celebration in the offing. 'Comanch' and me's not much for them fancy, sitting-down polite dinners. And, anyways, that blonde gal's setting up free drinks for us tonight at the saloon.'

'Mind you don't have too many of them,' Dusty ordered bluntly. Then he turned to Lampart and continued, 'I'd be right honoured to come, sir. Only I'd maybe best get these whiskers trimmed decent first.'

'No sooner said than done, *mon ami*,' le Blanc announced, darting a triumphant grin at the scowling Basmanov. Swinging on his heel, the barn's owner stalked from the room and the barber went on, waving to his chairs, 'If you and your brother will sit down, we'll attend to you. This time there shouldn't be any interruptions.'

'How do you read the sign on what happened in there, D – Ed?' the Kid asked half an hour later as he, Dusty and Waco strolled towards the hotel. 'Way I see it, the barber and his louse figured the Smiths'd be coming and saved your lives when they did.'

'Likely that's what Lampart told them to do,' Dusty replied. 'Only, was I you pair, I'd not count on it happening while I'm not with you tonight. It was me he wanted saving.'

'But le Blanc's boy twirled "Brother Matt" there around—' the Kid objected, recalling the conversation which had taken place, while he was having his hair cut and beard trimmed, discussing the shooting at length.

'And damned near twirled me too far,' Waco interrupted. 'Way I see it, there's not much goes on in Hell that Lampart doesn't get to hear about. You can bet he knowed the Smiths was sober enough to be figuring on coming after us. If he'd wanted us all dead, he'd've passed the word to let them get us. And he'd've warned us happen he'd wanted all three of us alive.'

'I'm with you so far,' admitted the Kid.

'Instead, he must've told le Blanc to keep watch and save just Brother Ed. They figured to let you take your chance, Comanch'; and to let Smith get me, but make it look like they'd tried to save me. If I'd've took lead, you'd likely've reckoned it was through the young feller spooking and turning the chair too hard.'

'That's about the size of it,' Dusty conceded.

'Just leave us have that young yahoo off somewheres quiet for a spell,' suggested the Kid, sounding as mild and innocent as was humanly possible. 'We'll soon know if your figuring's right or not.'

'Leave it be,' Dusty advised. 'We'll let them believe we're thinking the way they want us to. I reckon that Lampart's looking for backing against that Basmanov *hombre*. If so, given a mite of luck, I'll get him thinking that three of us're better than one. If we can get close to him, we can learn all there is to know about this town and how to bust it wide open.'

'We know one thing now,' Waco said soberly. 'They kill off fellers with rewards on their heads and get the bodies out to towns where they can collect the bounties.'

'We'd figured that much afore we got to Paducah,' commented the Kid.

'And we know for sure now,' Waco insisted. 'Toby Siddons was back-shot in town and buried here, 'cording to the barber's louse. It'd be mighty interesting to try opening up some more of those graves in boothill.'

'Don't try doing it tonight,' Dusty ordered. 'And watch how you go, boys. Basmanov might get somebody else to try and make wolf-bait of us, to stop us tying in with Lampart.'

CHAPTER NINE

I WAS SAWING MY WIFE IN HALF

Wearing his freshly-cleaned black Stetson, a frilly-bosomed white silk shirt, black string tie, grey town-fashion trousers tucked neatly into shining Wellington-leg boots and a Colt-laden gunbelt, Dusty Fog strolled into the hotel's dining-room. The time was just after ten o'clock in the evening of his first day at Hell. As the mayor had explained in a note which had been delivered to the small Texan, due to the rule prohibiting the lighting of fires during the hours of daylight, the dinner could not be prepared and served any earlier.

That afternoon, Dusty, the Ysabel Kid and Waco had made an extensive examination of the town and its surroundings. To avoid arousing suspicions as to their motives – cowhands being notorious for their dislike of walking – Dusty had given a reason publicly for their perambulations. While enjoying an excellent cold lunch at the hotel, he had announced in loud tones that he and his *amigos* would be taking a stroll that afternoon. So, happen any of Columbo's, Pinter's, Topple's or the Smith brothers' friends had the notion, the trio would be ready and available to accept objections.

The challenge had not been taken up. So Dusty, the Kid and Waco had conducted an enlightening survey of the area. Passing through the graveyard, they had located Toby Siddons' 'grave' and studied head-boards bearing the names of other outlaws. Half a dozen Mexicans and Chinese coolies had been digging holes to accommodate Columbo, Pinter, Topple and the Smith brothers. Walking on, Dusty had wondered if the men killed by himself and his *amigos* would occupy the graves. Or if the other corpses whose names appeared on the head-boards were really buried there.

Sixty or more adobe buildings were scattered around the wooden establishments on the street. Some were used by outlaws who probably objected to paying the hotel's high prices, or had been unable to obtain rooms in it. Others housed the Chinese and Mexicans who were employed to carry out various menial tasks in the town. The Kid had guessed that the latter were once slaves owned by the *Kweharehnuh* and traded, or given, to the citizens of Hell.

The discovery of six large wagons parked in three of the buildings had led the trio to make a closer scrutiny of the livery barn's corrals. They had found that a number of the horses were of a type bred for heavy haulage work. That had helped to explain how the town obtained its supplies.

One building in particular had aroused Dusty's interest. Situated about two hundred yards to the rear of the mayor's residence, it conveyed a similar impression of sturdiness. Small, cubic in shape, in an exceptional state of repair, its adobe walls had a single stoutly-made oak door, secured, like the heavily shuttered window, with double padlocks. Although Dusty had noticed the building while accompanying the Lamparts from the livery barn, he had not been aware of the full implications. The door and window were at the rear and on a bench under a shady porch, two Mexicans armed with shotguns kept watch on them. All the trio had wondered why the place should require a guard and Dusty had resolved to find out as soon as possible.

Ever curious, Waco had asked why the original settlers had selected such an inhospitable region for their home. The Kid had suggested that they were Spanish colonists. Adobe was a building material with lasting qualities and, apart from various repairs which had been carried out recently, the houses looked to be of considerable age. Going by the absence of a church, normally the first thing erected by the priest-ridden Spanish colonists, Dusty had concluded that the settlers had been non-believers driven by religious persecution to take refuge in the Palo Duro country.

Returning to the hotel at the conclusion of their inspection, the trio had exchanged gossip with le Blanc in the bar-room. Then they had gone to their rooms where they had rested and tidied up ready for the night's celebrations. Before coming downstairs, Dusty had given Waco and the Kid instructions as to how they were to act when they arrived at the saloon. By doing so, they would help him to convince Lampart that they too would be of the greatest use to him.

Like his equally duded-up companions, Dusty now sported a neatly-trimmed chin beard and moustache which he hoped would continue to serve as a disguise. Looking around the crowd of guests, he saw nobody whom he recognized from other towns and wondered if it would be mutual. Some of the male faces appeared to be familiar, but only because he had seen them on wanted posters. Others belonged to townsmen who had been at the livery barn that morning.

To Dusty, it was obvious that the citizens had started to form into two factions. Those who supported Lampart stood slightly apart from Basmanov's group. Although the mayor seemed to have the largest number on his side, Dusty guessed that some of them would be fence-sitting and waiting for a definite show of strength before declaring on his behalf. Having the backing of the acknowledged fastest gun in town would be tremendously in Lampart's favour. Which probably accounted for the way the mayor left his companion on seeing the small Texan arrive in the dining-room.

Although Dusty had devised an excuse for wearing his guns, he soon discovered that there would be no need for him to make it. Every man in the room, with the exception of Lampart, carried at least one revolver on his person.

'Ah, Edward!' the mayor greeted, coming over and extending his right hand. 'Let me introduce you to the other guests before my wife gets here.' He indicated a tall, handsome Mexican in an excellently tailored charro costume and wearing a low-hanging 1860 Army Colt with a set of decorative Tiffany grips. 'This is Don Miguel Santiago. You already know Jean here. These are Doctor Connolly, our medical practitioner, and our undertaker, Emmet Youseman.'

'I hope you can guess which of us is which,' boomed the big, red-faced, cheerful man in the loud check suit. 'In case you can't, I'm *not* the doctor.'

There was, Dusty decided, good cause for the comment. Tall, cadaverous and dressed in sober black, Doctor Connolly fitted the popular conception of an undertaker far better than the hearty, extroverted Youseman.

'It's looking the way I do that made me settle here,' the undertaker went on jovially, shaking hands with the small Texan. 'Fellers I get here don't have kin-folks to object. I reckon Doc helps my business. When a wounded feller sees him, he figures he's so close to the grave that he might's well go the whole hog and get into it.'

'It's no matter for levity,' Connolly declared in a high, dry voice and turned to walk away without acknowledging Lampart's introduction.

'Don't pay him no never-mind, Ed,' Youseman advised. 'He's riled because you boys gave me all the trade instead of him.'

'I'll mind it, happen I have to shoot anybody else,' Dusty promised. 'Only I've always been taught that any man who's acting bad enough for me to draw down on him is acting bad enough to be killed for it.'

Even as he finished speaking, Dusty realized that his words had come during a lull in the general conversation. Not that he regretted them for he realized that such a flat statement might do some good.

With the casual ease of an experienced host, Lampart steered Dusty onwards and rattled off other introductions. Nine of the men, like Santiago, could be found prominently – if not honourably – mentioned in the 'Bible Two', the Texas Rangers' annually published list of fugitives and wanted persons, which most peace officers in the Lone Star State read far more regularly than the original Bible. Wary eyes studied Dusty, but the greetings and handshakes were cordial until he reached the man who stood by Basmanov.

Tall, handsome, well-dressed, he had a pearl handled Colt Artillery Peacemaker in a fast-draw holster tied to his right thigh.

'And Andy Glover,' Lampart concluded.

'You're the *hombre* who dropped Ben Columbo, huh?' Glover growled, keeping his right hand at his side. 'Ben was real fast.'

'Sure,' Dusty conceded. 'There was only one thing wrong. Just the once, he wasn't fast enough.'

'Can't say I've heard your name,' Glover said sullenly, conscious that every eye had turned towards him and the small Texan.

'I've heard yours,' Dusty answered. 'Seen it on wanted posters, too. That's the difference between us, *Mr.* Glover. 'I've been too smart to get myself wanted until the stakes were worth it.'

'They say you robbed an Army Paymaster,' Glover gritted, not caring for the chuckles which greeted 'Caxton's' response. 'I've never known the blue-bellies sent their money about thataways.'

'Happen a secret gets known to too many folks, it stops being a secret,' Dusty countered. 'I just happened to have been in a position to get to know. That's how me and the boys managed to pull it off, *mister*. We knew where, when and how to do it.'

'And you're still on the dodge.'

'So're you, *mister*. Only I'm willing to bet that I brought in more money with that one robbery than you and your bunch were toting when you hit Hell.'

More laughter rose from the majority of the guests. It was common knowledge that, due to the Rangers' continual harassment, Glover's gang had been compelled to leave behind most of their loot. The bank robbery at Wichita Falls had been their last throw of the dice and had failed to come anywhere near their expectations in the amount of money it had produced. Dull red flooded into Glover's cheeks, but he had noted 'Caxton's' repeated use of the word 'mister'. No Texan said it after being introduced, unless he wished to show that he did not like the person he addressed it to.

'I see that you prefer the cross-draw, *senor*,' Santiago remarked. 'The same as Dusty Fog.'

'Why sure,' Dusty agreed, wondering if there might be some hidden meaning behind the Mexican's words. 'Fog's real fast, they do tell. So I figured the way he totes his guns must be something to do with it. That's why I wear them like I do.'

'Makes you fast, huh?' Glover muttered sullenly.

'Ben Columbo, Joey Pinter and Topple likely wondered that self same thing, *mister*,' Dusty drawled, looking straight at the big outlaw. 'They learned. If *anybody* feels so inclined to find out, I'm willing to step out on to the street and accommodate them.'

Gently spoken the words had been, but everybody present knew that they put the gauntlet straight into Glover's teeth. The remainder of the guests began to draw farther away, waiting silently to see what developed. Despite being the host, Lampart made no attempt to intervene. Nor did Basmanov, in his capacity as head of the Civic Regulators, do anything to try to keep the peace.

Almost thirty seconds ticked away, although they seemed to drag by for Glover. Much as he wanted to, the tall gang leader could not look away from his challenger. The *big* blond Texan's grey eyes held his own and appeared to be boring through and reading his innermost thoughts.

One thought beat at Glover. Before him stood the man who had simultaneously out-drawn and -shot Columbo and Joey Pinter, killing Topple an instant later. That put him into a class of *pistolero*-skill to which Glover could not hope to aspire. Yet if Glover backed down, he was finished in Hell. The story would be all around the town by morning and might even lose him the control he had previously exerted over the men in his gang.

Although determined to stand up against any man who tried to ride him, a good way to stay alive in such company, Dusty did not particularly want to kill Glover. So, having asserted himself, he sought for a way in which he might avoid taking the affair to a fatal conclusion. Sensing that Glover wanted to back off, Dusty saw an opportunity to let him do so. It had a certain amount of risk to the small Texan, but he felt sure that other issues swayed it in his favour.

Giselle Lampart stood at the open door, looking into the room. Jewellery sparkled at her fingers, wrists and neck, while the dress she wore leaned more to daring than decorous. Turning his back on Glover, Dusty swept off his Stetson with his left hand and walked towards the brunette.

'Good evening, ma'am.' the small Texan greeted, his whole attitude suggesting that he regarded the incident with Glover closed. 'My thanks for your kind invitation.'

Sucking in a deep breath of mingled anger and relief, Glover glared after the departing Texan. The outlaw's right hand hooked talon-like over its revolver's butt, almost quivering with anticipation as he tried to decide whether to draw or not. Commonsense, and a knowledge of the other guests' feelings, supplied him with the answer. If he started to pull the gun, one of his rivals might warn 'Caxton'. In fact, somebody was certain to do it for Glover's action would endanger Giselle Lampart. Given the slightest hint of what Glover was planning, 'Caxton' would turn to deal with the situation. Glover could not forget the *big* Texan's earlier comment on how he would treat any man who made him draw.

'Come and sit down, Andy,' Basmanov said in a loud voice. 'We don't want any unpleasantness.'

Never had the Russian barn owner's voice sounded so delightful to Glover. Yet the outlaw could sense a tinge of disappointment in it. Refusing to let that disturb him, he swung on his heel and walked with Basmanov to the long table which had been laid for the dinner.

'It looks as if nobody feels inclined to find out, Edward,' Giselle remarked with a mischievous smile. 'You may escort me to the table. I've had you placed next to Simmy and myself so that I will have a handsome man on each side of me.'

The tension had oozed away with the entrance of the brunette and Glover's retreat. Talk rose again and there was a general movement in the direction of the table. Guided by Giselle, Dusty went to the end of the table presided over by her husband. On the other end, Basmanov stood scowling from Dusty to the mayor. Going by the knowing looks thrown at him from various gang leaders, Dusty sensed that he was being awarded a place of honour. Perhaps the last time the Lamparts had given a dinner, Ben Columbo had occupied it. Dusty refused to let that thought worry him. To his left were Giselle and her husband, with Santiago on his right and le Blanc facing him across the table.

Moving with well-trained precision, Goldberg's Mexican waiters started to serve the meal. The food and wine proved to be of excellent quality, which did not surprise Dusty in the light of what he had already seen around the hotel. Soon conversations were being carried on and laughter rolled out. Although apparently at ease, Dusty remained constantly alert. Carefully he guided the talk in his group to the presence of the town in the Palo Duro.

'That was Simeon's doing,' le Blanc declared. 'Why not tell Ed how it happened, Simmy?'

'There's not much to tell,' the mayor replied, in a mock depreciatory tone and went on in a matter-of-fact manner. 'The first time the *Kweharehnuh* saw me, I was sawing my wife in half.'

'Huh?' Dusty grunted, genuinely startled.

'That's right, Ed,' Giselle confirmed. 'And it wasn't the first time. He'd done it to me twice a night for years.'

'You're a magician!' Dusty ejaculated, staring at Lampart with a growing understanding.

'One of the best, if I say so myself,' the mayor agreed. 'A most useful talent, I've always found it. And never more so than that night. We, the present citizens of Hell, were on a wagon train making its way down from the railroad in Kansas to Santa Fe. Our scout rode in to say that we were surrounded by Indians and they would attack our camp at dawn. We wouldn't have stood a chance in a fight, so I decided to try something else. Luckily I had all my props along. So Giselle and I put on our entire performance by fire- and lamplight. Of all my extensive repertoire, sawing Giselle in half went down the best. Ten Bears had never seen anything like it—'

'Or me, the way I dressed for the act,' Giselle put in, eyeing Dusty in a teasing manner.

'The whole band came down to watch,' Lampart continued. 'Next day, instead of attacking, they brought the medicine woman to see and, I suspect, explain the miracle. When she couldn't, Ten Bears decided that I must have extra powerful medicine and made me his blood-brother. After that, getting permission for us to make our homes here was easy.'

'Don't you want to know *why* we chose to settle here, Ed?' asked Youseman, sitting between the mayor and the barber.

'I figure that, happen he reckons it's my business, Mr. Lampart'll tell me about it,' Dusty replied, guessing that no further information would be forthcoming right then.

'I always feel so immodest when I talk about it,' Lampart remarked, placing a hand over his glass as the wine-waiter offered to fill it. 'No more for me, thank you.'

'If a man's done something as smart as starting this town, I don't see why he needs be that way about telling it,' Dusty praised. 'Fact is, the only modest fellers I've ever met are that way because they've never done anything and don't have any other choice.' He looked up and shook his head at the wine-waiter. 'I'll pass this deal, *amigo*.'

'You don't drink much, Edward,' Giselle commented. 'Aren't you enjoying yourself with us?'

'I'm having a right fine time, ma'am,' Dusty answered. 'Only I figure a man who has to pour liquor down his throat to enjoy himself doesn't have much to enjoy.'

'You object to people drinking, *senor*?' Santiago inquired, but in a polite and friendly manner.

'I object to *me* drinking,' Dusty corrected, hoping that somebody would take the bait. 'What other fellers do is none of my never-mind.'

'From the way your brother talks,' Lampart put in, just as Dusty had hoped, 'I don't think he shares your views.'

'Matt talks better than he drinks,' Dusty replied, taking the chance to impress the mayor with the Kid's and Waco's sterling qualities and the fact that they would be of use to him. 'They're good kids, him and Comanch' both. As loyal as they come and they always do just what I tell them. Tell you what, gents, I said they should stay sober tonight. And I'll bet a thousand dollars they're that way if we go along to the saloon when we're through here.'

'With Emma handing out the free drinks?' le Blanc laughed. 'You have much faith in them, *mon ami*.'

'Enough to make it five thousand dollars they'll still be sober,' Dusty offered, watching Lampart out of the corner of his eye and seeing him give a quick confirmatory nod to the barber.

'You are on, *mon brave*,' le Blanc declared, thrusting his right hand across the table. 'Who will hold the stakes?'

'Anybody who suits you,' Dusty said indifferently. 'I don't care who I get the money off.'

'You are so sure of winning then, Edward? Giselle asked.

'So sure that I'd go up to ten thousand simoleons on it,' Dusty declared, apparently addressing le Blanc, but actually watching the mayor's reaction.

'Not with me,' le Blanc chuckled, as he received a negative head-shake from Lampart. 'Against such confidence, I almost whish I had not made the wager.'

'Call it off, you feel that way,' offered Dusty. 'I know those boys and you-all don't.'

'No,' the barber decided, after another glance in the mayor's direction had told him what to do. 'We shook hands on it, so the bet is on. Besides, I too have faith. In Emma's hospitality and persuasive powers. We will see what happens when we get to the Honest Man. But who holds the stakes?'

'Mr. Lampart'll suit me fine,' Dusty stated. 'That way, he can put your money straight into my box in his office after I've won.'

CHAPTER TEN

IF YOU WASN'T WEARING THEM GUNS

'Ed Caxton!' Emma Nene said accusingly, bearing down on Dusty as he entered the Honest Man Saloon with Lampart, le Blanc and Santiago. 'What have you told those two boys of yours?'

With the dinner at an end, the party had started to split up and go their separate ways. First to leave had been Basmanov's faction, including the scowling, still angry Glover. Dusty had noticed that two of the men who had been with the Russian earlier stayed behind. Others, whom the small Texan had marked down as fence-sitters, showed a more open friendship towards Lampart. Already, it seemed, the fact that the mayor was apparently winning the support of 'Ed Caxton' was bringing its rewards.

There had been some after-dinner talk, then the men had decided to make their way to the saloon. Clearly Lampart had no intention of allowing his rival to make friendly advances towards Dusty and intended to reduce the chances of a successful attempt to assassinate the small Texan. The mayor had asked Dusty, along with le Blanc and Santiago, to be his guests at the saloon after they all had escorted Giselle home.

For all the deficiencies of its sign-board, the Honest Man Saloon came up to the high standard set by the rest of the town. On a dais at the left side of the room, the piano which had guided Dusty, the Kid and Waco to Hell combined with three guitars, two violins and a trumpet to beat out a lively dance rhythm. Before the dais was a space left clear for dancing. At the moment of Dusty's arrival, it was

97

hidden behind a wall of laughing, cheering Mexicans, members of Santiago's gang. Several pretty, shapely girls, white, Mexican and Chinese, in no more scanty attire than would be seen at a saloon in a normal town, mingled with the sixty or so male customers. Behind the bar counter, two Mexicans and a burly, heavily moustached white man served drinks from the extensive range of bottles gracing the shelves of the rear wall. Mexican waiters glided about carrying trays. Two tiger-decorated faro layouts, a chuck-a-luck table, a wheel-of-fortune and three poker games catered for the visitors who wished to gamble. At each end of the bar, a flight of stairs led up to the first floor.

Clearly Emma Nene did not apply the almost sedate clothing standards to herself. She wore a flame-coloured dress with an extreme décolleté which left no doubt that all under it was flesh and blood, and which clung to her magnificently feminine body like a second skin. Its hem extended to her feet, but was slit up the left side to the level of her hip. One leg, made more sensual by a covering of black silk, showed through the slit in a tantalizing manner. Her eyes held a puzzled, yet admiring, expression as she addressed the small Texan.

'How do you mean, ma'am?' Dusty answered, although he could guess.

'I thought they'd be drinking me dry, seeing that I offered to pay and going by the way they talked,' Emma elaborated. 'Instead, they've only had a couple of whiskies apiece and won't take any more.'

'Oh no!' le Blanc groaned.

'Something wrong, Jean?' the blonde asked.

'It would seem that I have lost five thousand dollars,' the barber replied. 'Ed bet me that his friends would still be sober when we arrived.'

'They're that, sure enough,' Emma admitted. 'Are you fellers going to stand here all night, or come over and buy a girl a drink?'

'It'll be my pleasure to buy one for you, ma'am,' Dusty declared.

'Hey, Brother Ed!' Waco whooped, coming up with his left arm hooked around the waist of a pretty, red-haired girl. 'This here's Red and she reckons I'm the best-looking feller she knows.'

'She shows right good taste, boy,' Dusty grinned. 'Where's Comanch'?'

'Whooping up a storm over there with a right sweet lil *senorita*,' the youngster replied, waving a hand to the dancefloor. 'And me all this time thinking all he knowed was war-dances 'n' hoedowns.'

As the party made their way to the bar, Dusty looked through the gap in the Mexican crowd. Beyond them, the Kid and a vivacious girl of Latin blood were giving a spirited rendering of a *paso doble*. From the sounds let out by the onlookers, even Santiago's gang were impressed by the Indian-dark Texan's part in the performance.

'He sure dances pretty,' Dusty drawled. 'How're things going, boy?'

'Couldn't be better,' Waco enthused and nodded to the blonde. 'Soon's Miss Emma seed we wasn't wanting to drink, she called up Red and Juanita to see after us. This's sure one friendly lil town.'

'Looks that way,' Dusty admitted. 'Go have your fun, boy. Only keep minding what I told you.'

'Don't I always?' Waco grinned. 'Come on, Red gal. Let's go buck the tiger for a whirl.'

'You were right, Ed,' Lampart said, watching Waco depart with an air of calculating appraisal. 'It's fortunate that they survived the Smiths' treacherous attack.'

'Right fortunate,' Dusty agreed. 'Three sets of guns're better than one comes a fuss.'

'Do they *always* do as you tell them, Ed?' Emma inquired, signalling to the white bartender.

'They've found life's a whole heap easier if they do,' Dusty answered.

'Mr. Caxton's money is no good tonight, Hubert,' Emma informed her employee. 'Set the drinks up over at my table.' She smiled at the men. 'It's not ladylike to stand guzzling at the bar. Do you insist on other people doing everything you tell them, Ed?'

'Depends on who they are,' Dusty declared. 'I can take orders just as easy as giving them, provided I think the man doing the giving's smarter than me.'

Although Dusty spoke to the blonde, his words had been directed at Lampart and he knew that the mayor was taking them in.

'Such as who for instance, *mon ami*?' le Blanc challenged.

'Like I said, *anybody* who's smarter than me,' Dusty countered and looked around. 'This's some place you've got here, ma'am.'

'Why thank you, kind sir,' Emma smiled and led the way to a table on the right side of the room.

'Yes sir,' Dusty said, as if half to himself. 'I'd surely admire to be the man who made this whole town possible.'

'You'll be making me blush next,' Lampart warned, but he could not hide the pleasure he felt at the praise. 'Sit down. This is Emma's private table and reserved for the guests she says can share it with her.'

'Take the end seat, Ed,' the blonde offered. 'You're our guest of honour tonight, and deserve to be for ridding Hell of a bunch of murderous rats.'

Sitting down, Dusty watched the other men take their places. Emma seated herself around the corner from him and Lampart sat opposite to her with his back to the wall.

'Pup-Tent Dorset's bucking the tiger, Miss Emma,' the bartender said *sotto voce* as he set down a tray of drinks. 'He's losing heavy and getting riled.'

'Is Glover here?' the blonde asked, turning to glance around the room.

'Come in with Basmanov,' Hubert answered. 'They got a bunch up in one of the rooms for a game of poker.'

'Did Dorset talk to Glover before they went up?' Lampart put in.

'Him and Styles Homburg went over to ask for some money, what I could see of it,' Hubert replied. 'They talked for a spell over by the stairs. Funny thing though, Glover made 'em hand over their guns afore he gave them a stake.'

'Dorset and Homburg are always poor losers,' Emma commented, after the bartender had returned to his duties. 'Oh ho! They're coming over here now.'

Turning his head, Dusty studied the two men who were approaching from the faro layout to which Waco had taken the saloon-girl. Pup-Tent Dorset was slightly over medium height, moustached, with a stocky, powerful build. Dressed in plain range clothes, his gunbelt's holster was empty. Bigger, bulkier, Styles Homburg looked like a sedate travelling salesman in a brown town suit. He too appeared to be unarmed.

After studying Dorset and Homburg, Dusty darted a quick glance around the room. The dance had ended and the Kid was taking Juanita through the laughing, applauding Mexicans to join Waco at the faro table. From his friends, the small Texan turned his attention to locating possible enemies. At the bar, standing clear of the other customers, he located the remainder of the Glover gang. Tommy Eel, tall, slim and tough-looking, leaned by the shorter, heavier, surly-featured Saw Cowper. Each of them had a revolver holstered at his right side.

'Hi, boys,' Emma greeted, in her professionally cordial manner, as the two outlaws came to a halt at her table. 'Can I help you?'

'Not you,' Dorset replied and pointed at Lampart. 'Him. We want some money from you, *hombre*.'

'In that case, I would suggest you go and ask Mr. Glover,' the mayor advised. 'He holds the only keys to your gang's box.'

'And you know just how little's in it,' Homburg growled. 'Not enough for us to have another week here. So we reckon you should ought to do something about it.'

'You can hardly blame me for your extravagances,' Lampart pointed out. 'I warned you on the day you arrived that this was an expensive town.'

'And took a tenth of our loot,' Dorset spat out. 'So we figure we're entitled to some of it back.'

'I don't, in fact can't, see it that way,' Lampart protested, aware that he was the focal point of much attention.

Silence had fallen on the room. The band had stopped playing, conversations ceased and various games of chance were temporarily forgotten as the customers and employees turned their gaze to Emma's table.

'What's that mean?' demanded Dorset.

'I told you when you first arrived that it was a donation to the Civic Improvement Fund,' Lampart explained. 'If I hand some of your donation back, I'll be expected to do the same with everybody who asks.'

'We said we wanted to borrow—' Dorset began.

'And meant you wanted a gift,' the mayor interrupted. 'Where could you get money to repay me?'

'We'd maybe win it, was the games in here straight,' Dorset answered, seeing that the crowd sympathized with Lampart's point and hoping to turn them in his and Homburg's favour.

'Are you sore-losers trying to say my games aren't honest?' Emma challenged indignantly.

'*Your* games?' Dorset sneered. 'Word has it you don't but run this place all cosy and loving for Lampart. And him with a nice, sweet lil wife, for shame.'

Wood squeaked against wood as Dusty sent his chair skidding back. Coming to his feet, he faced the two men.

'Was you wanting to stay healthy,' the small Texan drawled, 'you'd best say "Sorry we lied about you, ma'am." and then get the hell out of here.'

'Wha—?' Dorset began.

'You got business with Mr. Lampart, that's fine,' Dusty continued. 'Only some'd say you've picked a poor time to come doing it. It stops being fine when you start mean-mouthing and lie-spouting about a for-real lady. So I'm telling you to wear out some boot-leather walking away.'

'Lampart's hired your gun, huh?' Homburg almost shouted, recollecting the orders Glover had given regarding the pair's behaviour.

'If Glover told you that, he's as big a liar as you pair,' Dusty countered. 'And I'm getting quick-sick of seeing your faces.'

'You're the feller who dropped Ben Columbo, ain't you?' said Dorset. 'That makes you a real big man.'

'Talking pretty won't make me like you,' Dusty warned.

'Could be you wouldn't be so big,' Dorset declared, 'if you wasn't wearing them guns.'

'Now there's an interesting thought,' Dusty answered, starting to unfasten the pigging thongs which held the tips of his holsters to his legs. 'You figure happen I was to take them off, you could make me eat crow?'

For a moment, Dorset stood dumbfounded by the unexpected turn of events. He was uncertain of what he should do next. Then he realized what a chance was being presented to him and he nodded eagerly.

'That's just what I think!'

'And now you got all these good folks wondering if it be true,' Dusty continued as he unbuckled and laid his gunbelt on the table. 'So we're just natural' going to have to find out.'

'You fixing to take on me or Styles?' Dorset grinned.

'You, him, or both,' Dusty confirmed. 'Call it any way you've a mind.'

'I reckon I'll be enough,' Dorset declared, the grin fading away. 'Come ahead, short-stuff. This I'm going to enjoy.'

Clenching his fists, Dusty adopted the kind of stance favoured by the professional pugilists of the day. At least, he positioned his hands and arms in the conventional manner. His feet formed a 'T' position, the right pointing to the front and, a shoulders' width away, the left directed outwards. By bending his knees slightly, he distributed his weight evenly on the balls of his feet.

Throwing a grin at Homburg, Dorset moved towards Dusty. An experienced fist fighter, the outlaw watched Dusty's hands for a hint of how he planned to attack. At the same time, Dorset stabbed his right at the blond's face. Weaving his torso aside and letting the blow hiss by his head, Dusty swung his left foot around and up.

Concentrating on Dusty's hands, the kick took Dorset by surprise. Caught in the groin, he might have counted himself fortunate in that Dusty had not been able to build up full power while making the attack. As it was, pain caused him to double over and retreat. Gliding closer, Dusty hooked his knotted left fist into the outlaw's descending face. Lifted upright, Dorset was wide open for the continuation of his small assailant's assault. Hearing footsteps approaching from his rear, Dusty hurled across his right hand. Hard knuckles landed on the side of Dorset's jaw, sending him spinning and reeling back to the faro table he had recently quit. Landing on it, he scattered markers, coppers, money and cards in all directions.*

Even as Dusty knocked Dorset away, he felt himself gripped by the shoulders from behind. Giving a lifting heave, Homburg hurled the small Texan towards the bar. At first Dusty could do nothing to halt himself as the savage propulsion caused him to turn in Homburg's direction and run backwards. So far, the big outlaw had not followed him; which proved to be a foolish omission. Waiting until he had regained control of his equilibrium, Dusty seemed to tumble backwards. A concerted gasp rose as he went down, mingling with Homburg's yell of triumph. Then the man started to rush forward, with the intention of stomping Dusty into the floorboards.

Spitting out a mouthful of blood, Dorset sank until his left knee touched the floor. His right hand went to and started to draw a knife from its sheath in the top of his right boot. The blade came clear, but its owner was given no chance to use it. Powerful fingers clamped on to his right wrist and the scruff of his neck. Then his trapped arm was twisted behind his back and he felt himself being dragged until he leaned face-down on the table once more.

Unlike the majority of the crowd, the Kid felt no concern over the sight of Dusty toppling backwards. He was aware that the small Texan possessed considerable acrobatic agility. In part, it had been developed as a precaution against injury if he should be thrown when taking the bed-springs out of bad horses' bellies. It had also served him well while receiving instruction in the fighting skills which did so much to offset his lack of inches when dealing with larger, heavier men. Down in the Rio Hondo, working as Ole Devil Hardin's personal servant, lived a small man thought by many to be Chinese. While undeniably Oriental, Tommy Okasi insisted that he

* A more detailed description of a faro game is given in *Rangeland Hercules*.

came from some place called Nippon. To Dusty, he had
handed on the secrets – all but unknown at that period outside Japan – of *ju-jitsu* and *karate*. Learning how to fall
had been an important and vital lesson. So the Kid expected Dusty to avert the danger of the stomping, probably
in a spectacular manner. He was not disappointed.

Breaking his fall on his shoulders as Tommy Okasi had
taught him, Dusty rolled into a ball. Then, with a surging
thrust, he uncoiled and catapulted back to his feet. The action took Homburg by surprise, just as the kick had
Dorset, and he was granted as little opportunity to recover.
Ducking under Homburg's belatedly grabbing hands,
Dusty wrapped his arms around the outlaw's thighs, just
above the knees. Drawing the legs together, Dusty exerted
all his not inconsiderable strength and straightened up. He
lifted Homburg from the floor, heaving the man backwards. Coming down flat-footed and with his legs still not
parted, the impact against the floor-boards knocked him
breathless and witless.

Bounding after the man, Dusty sprang into the air.
Tilting back until his body was horizontal, he hurled the
soles of his boots full into the centre of Homburg's chest.
Hurtling across the room, the outlaw crashed through the
bat-wing doors. He barely touched the sidewalk while
crossing it and sprawled face down on to the hard-packed
surface of the street.

Maintaining his twin grips, Waco kept up the pressure
on Dorset's trapped arm until the hand opened and
released the knife. With that accomplished, the youngster
transferred his other hand to the outlaw's collar, jerked
him erect and thrust him away.

'Go pick on Broth—' the youngster began.

Catching his balance, Dorset spun around and hurled a
punch to the side of Waco's head. Twirling on his heels,
the youngster landed back-down on the table. Instead of
turning to Dusty, the outlaw leapt closer to the young
blond. Grabbing hold of Waco's throat, Dorset hauled
him up and started to choke him.

At the bar, Eel and Cowper had been watching the
developments with a growing sense of alarm. When they

J. T. Edson

saw Dusty leap up and kick Homburg backwards, while Waco was disarming Dorset, the pair knew that they must help carry out their boss's orders. They also decided that bare-handed tactics were not for them. Moving away from the bar, they started to reach for their guns.

Instantly a menacing figure seemed to just appear in front of them. It wore a grey shirt, string tie, town trousers and Indian moccasins; the white man's attire being topped by the savage features of a Comanche warrior on the look-out for a coup-counting.

Having been certain that Dusty could deal with Homburg, the Kid had kept the other two members of the Glover gang under observation. When they made their move, he stepped in fully ready to counter it.

'I ain't like Ed 'n' Matt, so I don't waste time with fool fist-fighting,' the Kid warned and the Dragoon in his right hand seemed to vibrate with homicidal eagerness. 'You want to side your *amigos*, shed your guns and go to it. But, happen your pleasure's shooting, I'll be right willing to oblige.'

Although partially dazed by the blow, Waco threw off its effects fast. Placing his palms together, he thrust them up between Dorset's arms. Snapping the hands apart, he knocked the fingers from his throat. Then he bunched his left fist, dropped his shoulder behind it and ripped a straight-arm punch to the centre of Dorset's face. Nostrils spurting blood, the outlaw blundered backwards across the room.

Landing from his leaping high kick, Dusty turned and saw Waco's predicament. Before the small Texan could go to his *amigo*'s assistance, Waco escaped and put Dorset into retreat. As Dorset came towards him, still going backwards, Dusty interlaced his fingers. Looking like a baseball batter swinging for a home run, Dusty pivoted and smashed his hands into the man's kidney region. Agony contorted Dorset's features as the blow arrived. He arched his back and stumbled helplessly in the direction from which he had come. Leaping to meet him, Waco hurled a power-packed right cross. With a solid 'whap!', the youngster's knuckles struck Dorset's temple. The outlaw pitched sideways and slid several feet before coming to a stop.

'How do you want it?' the Kid demanded as Dorset's limp body came to a halt. 'Now's the time to say.'

'Pup-Tent and Styles called the play,' Eel replied. 'It's none of our fuss, feller.'

Glover stood with Basmanov and others of the poker game on the right side set of stairs. Glaring furiously at the scene, the gang leader advanced a couple of steps below his companions. Drawing his revolver, he started to line it at the small Texan.

CHAPTER ELEVEN

HE'S GOT A FORTUNE STASHED AWAY

The crash of a shot sounded over the excited chatter which had followed the unexpected ending of the fight. On the stairs, Glover heard the eerie sound of a close-passing bullet, felt its wind on his face and gave a startled yelp. Jerking back in an involuntary motion, he sat down hard. Across the room, at Emma Nene's private table, smoke curled from the barrel of Santiago's Colt.

'What is the betting that I won't miss a second time?' asked the *bandido*, taking a more deliberate aim as he cocked the revolver's hammer.

Fright flickered on Glover's face, for he knew that his life had never been in greater danger. If anybody offered to bet, the Mexican would not hesitate to shoot. For a moment, Glover thought of trying to turn his weapon on Santiago. Yet doing so would avail him but little. Even if he should be successful, the *bandido*'s men would kill him. Covered by 'Comanche Blood's' Dragoon, Eel and Cowper would be unable to back his play. Nor could he count on help from Basmanov's party. That had been made plain to him during the poker game. As the Russian had warned, Glover's future in Hell depended upon how the plan worked that had been hatched between them after leaving the hotel. From what Glover had seen since coming downstairs, it had been a miserable failure.

'Easy there, Mig!' Glover said, trying to keep his voice firm and friendly. He dropped his gun. 'What was I to think when I come down and see the Caxtons beating up

one of my boys and Blood there holding the others back
with a gun.'

'Put up your gun, *amigo*,' Dusty agreed, going to the
table and picking up his belt. 'Man's right about the way it
looked. Trouble being, things aren't always how they
look.' Once more silence had come to the room and its occupants listened to his words with rapt attention. 'No sir.
Take when them two yacks of his came over. Way they
talked and acted, it could've looked like I'd been hired by
Mr. Lampart to stop folks getting their right and fair
money out of his office.'

'That was the impression they tried to give,' Santiago
confirmed.

'Some's say they was lucky, them two, that their boss'd
taken their guns away—' Dusty went on.

'I could see they was getting riled over losing at faro,'
Glover interrupted, standing up. 'So I did it for the best.'

'Why sure,' Dusty agreed. 'It looks that way. Only you
could've got them both killed, doing it.'

'How?' Glover growled.

'Would Ben Columbo or Joey Pinter've taken off their
guns to deal with them?' Dusty challenged. 'And if I
hadn't, when I concluded to stop them mean-mouthing
Miss Emma with their lies about her and her games, folks
might've seen it wrong. They might start to figure –
'specially was somebody to put it into their heads—' his
eyes flickered briefly at Basmanov, 'that I was working for
Mr. Lampart and the other gents with money in his care
could wind up dead when they wanted it back.'

A startled exclamation in his native tongue broke from
Basmanov as he heard Dusty exposing his plot. Not only
exposing it, but doing so in such a manner that nothing
could be salvaged from it.

Glover had been willing to sacrifice Dorset and Homburg in the interests of raising mistrust against the mayor.
Far from the most intelligent of men, the pair had been
persuaded to hand over their guns and then provoke a fight
with 'Ed Caxton'. There had been a chance that he would
grand-stand, to impress Lampart and Emma Nene, by
agreeing to fight bare-handed. The conspirators, however,

had felt it more likely that he would shoot his challengers down regardless of them being unarmed. If Eel and Cowper had been able to avenge their companions by killing 'Caxton', all well and good. If not, Basmanov would be able to circulate the kind of rumour that the small Texan had suggested.

Instead of achieving their ends, the whole affair had gone wrong. Worse than that. Basmanov sensed that the *big* dangerous newcomer suspected his part in the scheme.

'Put that blasted hand-cannon away, Comanch',' Dusty commanded, having completed the buckling on of his belt and secured its holsters to his legs while apparently addressing Glover but really speaking to the crowd, 'Those two fellers only want to tend to their *amigos'* hurts.'

'Yo!' answered the Kid and obeyed.

'Do it,' Glover said as Eel and Cowper glanced at him. 'You'd best have Doc Connolly see to them, they could be hurt bad.'

'Hank,' Dusty called, to a gang leader who wore the clothes favoured by professional gamblers. 'Just to straighten out any doubts them two yacks might have stirred up, will you check over that faro lay-out.'

'I've done it every night,' the man replied. 'It's like all the games in here, as straight as Emma's beautiful.'

'You saying things like that about the lady, I reckon I'd best ask you to show Mr. Glover and his boys what to look for in a crooked game,' Dusty grinned. 'Fancy-talking competition like yours, I can do without. 'Course, they might not want to take your word on it.'

'Hank knows what he's talking about and what he's said's good enough for us,' Glover growled, picking up and holstering his revolver. 'Pup-Tent and Styles was allus poor losers. So I took their guns off 'em, to stop them making trouble if their luck stayed bad.'

'Like I said, they was lucky you did it,' Dusty drawled. 'Only, happen they come mean-mouthing or spreading lies about Emma again, I'll not waste effort fist fighting. And that goes whether *they're* wearing guns or not.'

'That Dorset *hombre's* got a real hard head,' Waco went on, alternately rubbing his right hand's knuckles and working its fingers. 'Happen we lock horns again, I'll be inclined to hit him with a teensy bit of lead 'stead of my dainty lil fist.'

'We'll mind it,' Glover promised sullenly. 'Come on, Tommy, Saw. Let's get the boys to the doctor's.'

'Hey, you musicians!' Emma called. 'Earn your pay. Come on, fellers, you'll put me in the poor-house, sitting on your hands instead of buying or playing.'

Taking their cue from the blonde, the band started to play a lively tune. Girls and waiters set about stimulating the activities which had been brought to a halt by the trouble. By the time Glover, Eel and Cowper had carried Dorset from the room, it reverberated with the sound of revelry.

'Where-at's Emmet Youseman?' Dusty inquired. 'Don't tell me he's undertaking at this hour of the night?'

'I shouldn't think so,' Lampart answered looking a touch furtive.

'He didn't strike me as a feller who'd miss the chance to bend an elbow in good company,' Dusty remarked, flickering a glance at Waco.

'Most likely he's doing some undertaking at the cathouse,' le Blanc remarked. 'Only with live customers.'

'Where's Red got to?' Waco whooped and the girl ran up. Scooping her in his left arm, he kissed her. 'I thought you'd backed out, gal.'

'What on?' Emma demanded.

'Why, I've bet her that I've got more hair on my chest than she has,' the youngster explained. 'And, happen it's all right with you, Miss Emma, I was figuring on taking her out for a whiles to show for most.'

'I told you that Red was your gal,' Emma reminded him. 'Run along and get your bet settled.'

'You heard the boss-lady, Red gal,' Waco grinned. 'Let's go.'

'What it is to be young,' Emma smiled, almost wistfully, watching Waco and the girl making for a side door.

'Aren't you going to fix Ed up with a girl, Emma?' le Blanc asked.

'I already have,' the blonde stated. 'Come on, let's set

the paying customers a good example. Sit down and get happy.'

'Let's do that,' Dusty agreed. 'I sure hope that gal of mine's a blonde.'

'You know,' Emma replied. 'She just might be at that.'

Although the party sat down and resumed their conversation, the subject of the motives behind the fight received no discussion. In fact, to Dusty it seemed that Lampart was trying to avoid it. The mayor kept the others laughing with a flow of rude stories. When he ran out, he offered to demonstrate a few of the tricks he had learned as a stage magician.

'You're not sawing me in half,' Emma warned.

'Spoil-sport,' Lampart chuckled. 'Get me a couple of decks of cards, I may be able to baffle you.'

Dusty had to admit that Lampart was a skilled performer. Handling the cards with deft professionalism, he kept his audience baffled. Emma had been asked to sing a song and was on her way to oblige, while Lampart concluded his show by demonstrating how to shuffle a deck of cards in each hand, when Glover returned.

'Look, Simmy, I don't want to bother you,' the outlaw said as he came to the table. 'But I need some money to pay Doc Connolly. The boys aren't the only ones who lost tonight.'

'Very well,' Lampart replied.

'I wasn't fixing to ask,' Dusty drawled, 'but seeing's you've got to open your office, I'll come and get myself a stake. There's a diamond bracelet down to the jewellery store that'd just do fine for a birthday present.'

'Who for?' le Blanc smiled.

'Not my mother, you can count on that,' Dusty grinned back.

'You know the rules, Andy,' Lampart said. 'I have to have a member of the Civic Regulators with me if I open the office after dark.'

'Mr. Basmanov's upstairs,' Dusty hinted.

'So he is,' agreed Lampart. 'Why should he sit gambling and carousing when I've got to work. Ask him if he'll come with us, will you please, Jean?'

'With the greatest of pleasure,' Le Blanc responded and went to do so.

By the time a scowling Basmanov had arrived, Emma was coming to the end of her somewhat ribald song. Acknowledging the applause, she left the dais and walked back to her table. On being told that Dusty would be leaving, she extracted his promise to return as soon as possible.

'Tommy'll have to come along,' Glover said, indicating Eel standing on the sidewalk as the men emerged from the saloon. 'He's got the other key to our box.'

'That's all right with me,' Lampart comfirmed, but he caught Dusty's eye and shook his head briefly. 'Where's Mr. Cowper?'

'Down to the doctor's,' Glover replied. 'You stove in three of Styles Homburg's ribs when you jumped up and kicked him, Ed.'

'Feller who taught me to do it allowed that could happen,' Dusty answered disinterestedly. 'How's the other one?'

'Still unconscious,' Eel put in. 'His head's broke, the doctor says.'

'They called the play,' Dusty reminded the outlaws.

'Nobody's gainsaying it,' Glover grunted.

Approaching the mayor's house, Dusty saw a glint of light showing through a crack in the curtains at the window of the mayor's office. He recollected his host having mentioned that the room was kept illuminated all night as a precaution against attempted thefts.

Unlocking the front door, Lampart allowed the other men to precede him into the hall. A lamp hung in the centre of the ceiling, throwing its light over the party. Closing the door, the mayor went to his office.

'Come in, Andy,' he said, turning another key. 'You'll have to wait until I've dealt with these gentlemen, Ed.'

'That's all right with me, sir,' Dusty drawled. 'Just so long as I can get to the jewellery shop before it closes.'

'You'll do that easy enough,' Basmanov said, in a more friendly voice than he had previously employed. 'He stays open until daybreak. Fellers get generous to Emma and her girls late on. You don't need me in there, do you, Simmy?'

'No,' the mayor replied, but Dusty thought he detected an undercurrent of worry in the one word. 'I'll handle things.'

'What do you think of Simmy?' the Russian inquired as he and Dusty stood in the hall after the other three had disappeared behind the door of the office.

'I like him fine,' Dusty replied. 'He's a good man. Smart, too.'

'What with his cut from you fellers' loot, and the saloon's takings – he owns it, not Emma, you know,' Basmanov went on, 'he's got a fortune stashed away.'

'It says right in the Good Book that the labourer's worthy of his hire,' Dusty pointed out. 'Which I don't reckon any of you fellers who live here's wives need to take in washing to help buy your bacon and beans.'

'I admit it's profitable,' the Russian replied. 'But some are making more than the others.'

'Drop those guns!'

Muffled by the thickness of the walls and door, Lampart's shouted words came to Dusty's ears. They were followed by four shots which sounded as a very rapid roll of detonations.

'What the hell!' Basmanov spat out in Russian, leaping towards the door.

About to follow him, Dusty became aware of another factor entering the game. The front door flew open and Cowper burst in with a revolver held ready for use. At the sight of Basmanov, he seemed to hesitate. That cost him his life. Dusty's left hand had already commenced its movement towards his right side. Steel rasped on leather, being all but drowned as the off side Colt came from its holster, lined and crashed.

With his mouth opening to yell something, Cowper received a bullet between his eyes. Back snapped his head, while his feet continued to advance. The latter left the floor and the former struck it with a shattering thud which the outlaw did not feel.

'Watch that one!' Dusty barked, springing by Basmanov.

On trying the office's door, Dusty found it to be locked. Although he had kicked an entrance into a room on occasion, he doubted if he could do so with that sturdy door. Bare feet slapped on the floor at the rear of the passage. Clad in a robe donned hurriedly after leaving her bed, Giselle darted in. Skidding to a halt, she stared from the smoking Colt in Dusty's hand to the body lying half in and half out of the front door.

'What's—?' the brunette began.

'Do you have a key for this door?' Dusty demanded.

'No,' Giselle answered, with surprising calm under the circumstances. 'But why should—?'

'There's no other way out of it?' Dusty interrupted.

'Of course not!' Giselle declared. 'What is happening, Edward?'

'There's been some shooting in the office,' Basmanov explained. 'We want to get in to investigate.'

'You could try breaking down the door,' Giselle suggested, still not displaying any concern for her husband's safety.

'You'd best get some of the Regulators at the windows before we try it,' Dusty told the Russian. 'But if they've got Mr. Lampart alive, we're in trouble.'

At that moment, the lock clicked and the door opened. Instantly Dusty pushed Giselle along the passage with his right hand and lined the Colt with his left. Holding the revolver from his desk, Lampart stood in the doorway. Fear showed on his face as he found himself staring down the barrel of Dusty's gun.

'Hey!' Lampart yelped feebly.

'Are you all right, Mr. Lampart?' Dusty asked, lowering the revolver.

'Yes,' the mayor confirmed and looked relieved. He stepped back, pointing with his empty hand. 'I'm afraid I had to kill them both.'

Entering the office and holstering his Colt, Dusty looked around. Gripping a revolver in his right fist, Glover sprawled on his back. Blood oozed from the two holes in his chest. Eel hung face down along the line of boxes to the left of his boss, his gun on the floor and his back a gory mess where two bullets had burst out. Going closer, Dusty noticed that the hammer of each dead man's revolver was still at the down position and Glover's forefinger extended along the outside of the triggerguard. Two padlock keys lay in front of a box.

Allowing Basmanov and Dusty to make their examination of the office, Lampart went to his desk. He flopped into his chair and laid the revolver in its usual place. Walking over, Dusty leaned on the desk to place a hand upon the mayor's shoulder. At the same time, his other hand rested on the cold metal of Lampart's Colt.

'Are you all right, sir?' Dusty asked gently.

'Y – Yes,' Lampart answered. 'I had to do it, Ivan, Ed.'

'Likely you did, sir,' Dusty drawled. 'Best tell us all that happened.'

'We came in and I did as I always do when somebody is drawing out money, sat behind the desk here. They went to their box, then turned and drew their guns. I had to start shooting. It was them or me.'

'You did the right thing, sir,' Dusty declared. 'Don't you reckon so, Mr. Basmanov?'

'Yes!' grunted the Russian. 'But why would they try it?'

'They were almost out of money, 'ccording to what was said at the saloon,' Dusty pointed out. 'Taken with their *amigo* coming busting in at the front door, when he was supposed to be along at the doctor's place with them hurt fellers, I'd say it all points to them figuring on robbing Mr. Lampart.'

'I suppose so,' Basmanov admitted sullenly, aware that several people had arrived and were listening.

So was Dusty. Figuring that some of the arrivals would be outlaws, he went on. 'And not just Mr. Lampart. Had they got away with it, they'd've emptied all our boxes to take with them.'

'Without the keys?' Basmanov asked, trying to salvage something from the death of Glover.

'Why not?' challenged Dusty. 'They likely aimed to keep Mr. Lampart quiet while they bust the locks. It could be done without too much noise. Quietly enough not to be heard outside, anyways.'

Seeing that, for the time being at any rate, he could not use the incident in his campaign to unseat the mayor, Basmanov raised no further objections. Instead, he set about his duty as head of the Regulators and attended to the removal of the bodies.

Waco and the Kid had both been among the crowd, but, having satisfied themselves that Dusty was safe, they returned to the waiting girls. Listening to Red warn the young blond that she 'wouldn't go walking 'round no more creepy ole graveyards,' Dusty grinned. Clearly Waco had been trying to solve one of the mysteries which puzzled the trio. Then, seeing the possessive manner in which the girls clung to his companions' arms, he realized what was happening. Lampart was keeping 'Matt Caxton' and 'Comanche Blood' under observation in a way which would be unlikely to arouse their suspicion.

Having taken some money from his party's box, Dusty called at the jeweller's store and purchased the best diamond bracelet in his extensive stock. Then he went back to the saloon. Although Emma came straight over to ask what had happened and if he was hurt, Dusty did not find the opportunity to hand over his present until just before the place closed.

'For your birthday,' Dusty whispered, slipping the bracelet into her hand as they watched the other customers leaving.

'My—?' Emma gasped.

'This year's, or last's, whichever's closest,' Dusty explained.

'Why thank you, Ed!' the blonde purred. 'My, you did dirty your shirt in the fight. You can't wear it until it's been washed.'

'You want for me to change it down here?'

'Of course not. Come upstairs and I'll show you where you can do it.'

Going upstairs and to the rear of the building, Emma escorted him into the bedroom section of her quarters.

'Take it off and I'll have my maid wash it,' the blonde offered.

Removing his tie, Dusty peeled off the shirt. Emma took

it from him and left the room. She returned empty handed and her eyes roamed over his powerfully developed bare torso.

'Oh my!' she said, reaching behind her and unhooking her dress. 'Haven't I made a mistake? You can't walk out of here without a shirt.'

'What'll I do then?' Dusty inquired.

The dress slid away. All Emma wore under it was a pair of black silk tights.

'Can't you think of anything?' she asked.

'You know,' Dusty replied. 'I just might be able to at that.'

CHAPTER TWELVE

THEY WON'T TOUCH THAT BUILDING

'Whooee!' enthused the Kid as he and his companions exercised their horses on the fringe of the wooded country which surrounded the vast hollow that held the town of Hell. 'Ole Mark'd sure enjoy being here. Who won that bet, boy?'

'You mind your own blasted business!' the youngster ordered indignantly. 'Way your bed was a-creaking and a-groaning last night Red and me didn't hardly get any sleep.'

'What Juanita and me heard through the wall, you pair wasn't doing much of that sleeping anyways,' countered the Kid. 'Which I'm right grateful to you for the loan of your room, Ed.'

'Emma and me figured you might's well use it, seeing I'd paid for it and wouldn't be,' Dusty answered. 'So she sent her maid along with the key. Did you pair learn anything from the gals?'

'Only that I've got more hair on my chest than she has,' Waco grinned, then became more serious. 'They don't know anything much. Only that some gangs go and come back and others just come the once.'

'We already had that figured out,' Dusty said.

'I was fixing to take a *pasear* round the back of the undertaker's afore I went to bed,' the Kid stated. ''But those gals wouldn't go leave us long enough and I didn't take to the notion of climbing that fence back of the shop with Juanita hanging on my shirt-tail.'

'It can't be helped,' Dusty said philosophically. 'They

didn't leave me on my lonesome, either.'

'I talked to a couple of fellers who saw Columbo's bunch being planted,' Waco remarked. 'Can't say's I claim to know sic 'em about undertakering, but I don't reckon there'd've been time for ole Happy Youseman to've embalmed them afore he put them under.'

'I wonder if anybody saw them in the coffins?' Dusty replied.

'Maybe they've planted those *hombres* and don't aim to claim the bounty,' the Kid suggested. 'Just to still the talk.' He shook his head. 'If there's been any talk, I haven't heard it. And Columbo 'n' Pinter both're worth a damned sight more in reward money than Toby Siddons was.'

'When I asked, they reckoned Youseman was at the hawgranch,' Dusty pointed out. 'It could be.'

'Did Glover try to stick the mayor up, you reckon, Brother Matt?' Waco inquired, changing the subject.

'Could be,' Dusty replied. 'Couple of the Regulators found their horses, saddled and ready for travelling, around the back of the houses.'

'Was Basmanov in on it?' the Kid wanted to know.

'He may have known they planned something like it, suggested that they tried it even,' Dusty answered. 'But I don't reckon he was expecting it last night, or he wouldn't've come with us.'

'Maybe Glover just meant to collect his money from the box, then rob one of the other townsmen afore they lit out,' Waco suggested, selecting the true reason although he would never know it. 'With that cocked Colt on Lampart's desk, they'd know better than try it against him.'

'You'd figure they would,' Dusty agreed. Then he gave his companions a warning about that particular weapon, concluding. 'It's just a notion I've got, but keep it in mind. It could help keep you alive.'

'We'll not forget,' the Kid promised. 'Did you learn anything from Emma?'

'Nothing to help us,' Dusty admitted. 'But I got the feeling she wanted to tell me something. Could be she's got notions of how she'd rate around town with us three backing her play, only she's not sure how I stand with Lampart.'

'Talking about him,' Waco drawled. 'His missus's headed this way.'

'I'd a notion she might,' Dusty replied. 'They made sure we couldn't get together and talk in private last night and it looks like they figure to keep on doing it.'

Giselle's arrival, riding her dainty *palomino*, brought the trio's discussion to an end. However, they had managed to exchange some information – mostly negative – and, more important, Dusty had had the opportunity to warn his *amigos* about the revolver which always lay cocked and ready for use on Lampart's desk.

'I wish I'd known you meant to come riding, Edward,' Giselle said. 'I do enjoy taking Goldie here out, but Simmy prefers I have an escort.'

'We'll keep it in mind, ma'am,' Dusty declared.

Clearly Lampart did not intend letting Basmanov make an attempt to win 'Ed Caxton's' friendship. On returning from their ride, the trio found the mayor and le Blanc waiting at the stable with an invitation for them to go to lunch. The Russian watched them go, scowling and brooding, but made no comment and did not try to interfere.

Playing on Lampart's eagerness to impress him and his companions, and win their approbation, Dusty led him to talk about the town. The mayor had great pride in the community, or rather in his part in founding it. So he needed little prompting to divulge details of its history.

From what Lampart told them, Dusty, the Kid and Waco began to realize that the wagon train had been of a somewhat unusual nature. With the exception of the Lamparts and Orville Hatchet, their scout, every person on it had been a fugitive from justice. It had been Lampart who gathered them and arranged what should have been a safe passage to Mexico. Wishing to avoid coming into contact with peace officers, they had swung east of the regular route and so found themselves in danger of being massacred by the *Kweharehnuh*. The trio had already heard how that peril was averted and turned to Lampart's advantage. Beyond mentioning how he had possessed contacts who put him in touch with a prime selection of fugitives, Lampart had refused to give further information in le Blanc's presence.

The rest of the day passed quietly. In the afternoon, Hatchet, returned from 'buying supplies' in Paducah. Showing a lack of tact, Giselle told him that 'Comanche Blood' was responsible for the loss of his horse when he had been riding with the posse. No trouble came from the remark, for Hatchet claimed he knew who had done it and why.

Dusty and his *amigos* found no opportunity to hold a private discussion that day. The Lamparts kept them occupied until sundown, then Emma and the girls took over. Once again Dusty shared the blonde's bed. While she made passionate love to him, he sensed she wanted to take him into her confidence on some matter. However, they separated next morning without her doing so. He wondered if he should encourage her, or if he would be better employed in keeping Lampart satisfied with his loyalty. There was a chance that Emma had been told to learn his real feelings and report them to the mayor.

Due to the ruling about fires, the town tended to do most of its business at night. Consequently most of its residents and visitors slept late in the mornings. Dusty, the Kid and Waco were no exception to the rule.

Picking Giselle up at noon, the trio escorted her on a ride around the area. They were repaid by information when she mentioned that Hatchet had already left town to collect more supplies; and did not need an explanation of what that meant. On their return, they were invited to take a belated lunch with the Lamparts. As they were alone, the mayor expanded on the histories of the people who inhabited Hell.

Youseman had been a surgeon and Connolly's partner carrying out experimental research on the subject of longevity. Needing corpses to work on, they had dealt with New York body-snatchers. Then they had graduated to killing healthy people to obtain fresh blood, tissues and organs for their experiments. The law had got wind of their activities, causing them to flee for their lives. They had been able to produce sufficient money to buy places on Lampart's wagon train.

Le Blanc had been a fashionable barber in New York until he had fallen in love with the beautiful wife of an elderly millionaire. Not until he had killed her husband did he discover that she loved another man and had merely been using him. He had murdered the couple in jealous rage, but was cool enough to carry off a large sum of money and a valuable collection of jewellery they had obtained to use as a start to their new life. With no other avenue of escape open to him, le Blanc had been willing to accept Lampart's offer of transportation.

Goldberg and the jeweller had been prominent Wall Street brokers, manipulating the stock market for their mutual advantage. After they had organized a slump which ruined thousands of investors, they had been exposed by a Pinkerton agent planted in their office. Needing a safe haven for themselves and their ill-gotten gains, they had snapped up Lampart's offer of providing it.

Driven from Russia because of his political activities, Basmanov had soon been up to his old tricks in the United States. Along with other anarchist agitators, he had formed a society whose aims had been to overthrow the government and take control in the 'interests' of the people. They had extorted money from immigrants and their funds had been further swelled by donations from various 'liberal' associations. Unfortunately, one of their number had planted a bomb on a bridge, wrecking a train with a heavy loss of lives and drawing unwanted attention to their activities. Sensing the net tightening about him, Basmanov had betrayed his companions and absconded with their not-inconsiderable funds. He too had been drawn into Lampart's band of escaping criminals.

None of the other citizens had more savoury backgrounds, their activities covering everything from white-slaving to drug smuggling and mass murder. One thing they all had in common: they were rich enough to pay their way and live in comfort – providing the forces of law and order did not find them.

From acquainting his audience with the unworthy natures of his fellow citizens, Lampart went on to impress them with his own brilliance. On winning the confidence of the *Kweharehnuh* and hearing about the ruined village deep in the Palo Duro country, he had seen its possibilities. After some argument, he had brought the other travellers around to his way of thinking. They had become persuaded that not only would they be safer than in Mexico, but they could also make their accumulated money earn more while awaiting the day when it would be safe for them to show their faces in public again.

Between them, the travellers had possessed the finances needed to rebuild the town. Owing to his part in a bloody racial conflict, the owner of the Chinese laundry was wanted by the law. However, he was an influential member of his Tong and brought in coolies to help with the work of building. As the Kid had guessed, the Mexican peons were slaves purchased from the *Kweharehnuh*. When all was ready, Hatchet had passed the word around the outlaw trails of what the town had to offer. The news could not have been better timed. It had come just after the Rangers were reformed and they were striking hard, closing down many hide-outs used by the gangs.

From the beginning, Lampart had insisted on offering the visitors a high standard of service. Not only were the food and drinks of top quality, but the gambling games at the saloon were scrupulously honest. Considering that some of the players would be crooked gamblers capable of detecting any cheating method or device, the latter had been a wise precaution.

The high standard served a dual purpose, Lampart told the Texans. Scouts were posted to meet and check on the men who came to Hell, disarming them before guiding them in. That was to safeguard against protests when the outlaws learned they must hand over one tenth of their total loot if they wanted to stay. Lampart could point out the excellent amenities, and explain how much they cost, as an excuse for taking the money. Secondly, the quality went towards justifying the increased prices charged in the town. He stated that, after their first visit, none of the outlaws had raised objections to paying to the Civic Improvements Fund when they came again.

That, apparently, was as far as the mayor intended to go on the subject of the visitors. Guessing that they would not hear about the fate of the dead outlaws, the Kid had asked about Ten Bears' reaction to having white men passing through his territory. Lampart admitted that, at first, the chief had not been keen on the idea. A further display of magic, backed by the offer of a repeating rifle and ammunition for every brave in the band, had brought him to a more amenable frame of mind.

'Could be a mite risky giving all them bucks rifles and shells,' Waco warned. 'They might figure, having 'em, their medicine's stronger than your'n.'

'I made sure they know they'll only have luck as long as they use the guns to help me,' Lampart replied. 'And I only hand out fifty rounds a month to each man. I had one bit of good fortune. A war bonnet chief called Kills Something was getting restless. He borrowed bullets from other men to arm a war party. They ambushed a patrol, but something went wrong and he was killed. His party had used up a whole lot of ammunition, with precious little but dead and wounded to show for it. That's quietened the others down. They know there's no more bullets for them until the next new moon.'

'That's fine as long as you don't disappoint them when the time comes,' Waco said, catching the Kid's eye and wondering what he thought about having, inadvertently, helped Lampart to keep control of the *Kweharehnuh*.

'I can,' Lampart claimed. 'The shack behind the house is filled with ammunition, and they know it.'

'Maybe they'll figure on helping themselves afore the new moon,' Waco went on. 'Comanch' allows that *Nemenuh* brave-hearts can sneak a man's hoss from under him on a dark night, and him not know until he tries to ride off on it. Be they close to that good, they'd get by them fellers you've got guarding it.'

'They won't touch that building,' Lampart declared, with an air of self-satisfied confidence. 'I've made sure of that.'

'How?' asked the Kid.

'In two ways. I've had photographs of Ten Bears and the medicine woman taken. They think I've captured their souls and they'll be damned if I destroy the pictures. So they use their influence to keep the braves in hand.'

'Which's only one way,' Dusty hinted.

'When the first of the guns and ammunition arrived, I called a meeting with Ten Bears and his men,' Lampart obliged. 'I warned them that I'd put a curse on the whole consignment which would kill any man who tried to steal from me or harm my friends. Then I gave them a practical demonstration. I placed a keg of powder out in the centre of a large, bare patch of sand, stood fifty yards from it and told any brave who thought I was lying to try to fetch it back. Two took the challenge and the keg blew up when they reached it.' He paused and finished, 'Before they had even touched it at that.'

'You had a feller hid out and he put a bullet into it,' Waco guessed, knowing that the mayor wanted them to try to explain how he had worked the trick.

'Unless it had been fired from so far away that the man could barely see the keg, much less hit it,' Lampart replied, 'they would have heard the shot.'

'You couldn't've run a fuse out to the keg,' the Kid decided. 'The braves'd've known what you was up to when you lit it.'

'True enough, Comanche,' Lampart grinned. 'What do you think, Ed?'

'You used a wire fuse and a "magnetic" battery to set the keg off,' the small Texan stated, watching the mayor's face register mingled annoyance and admiration at his summation. 'I've heard tell of such, but never seen one used.'

'The Indians hadn't even heard tell of it,' Lampart announced. 'On the night before the meeting, I'd buried the wire and smoothed away all traces of it. Next day, while Giselle performed a special "medicine" dance around the box holding the battery, I carried the keg out to the wire.'

'The Indians were all watching me,' the brunette remarked. 'And, if you'd seen what I was wearing, you'd know why.'

'It distracted them all right,' Lampart agreed. 'None of them saw me find the wire and connect it to the detonator in the bottom of the keg. Then I came back, joined Giselle and we both made some "medicine" while I coupled up the other end to the battery. Misdirecting the audience is the basic part of a magician's trade. I got the braves to take up my challenge and set off the keg when they reached it. You can imagine what kind of effect that made.'

'Near enough,' Dusty agreed. 'But there's more to it, isn't there?'

'A little. I had Giselle do another dance around a second keg and let the Indians see me take it into the shack. Ten Bears and his braves believe it will explode if anybody tries to take it. And it will.'

'Now you've lost me,' Dusty admitted, guessing what was implied but hoping to gain more information.

'I've got that keg wired up to a battery in my desk,' Lampart explained, indicating the left side drawer. 'The moment one of my guards raises the alarm, Giselle or I come in here and touch it off.'

'You've sure got it all worked out slicker'n a hawg greased down for cooking,' the Kid praised inelegantly.

'Yes, sir,' Waco agreed, then grinned. 'No offence, sir, and with all respect, ma'am, I'd sure admire to see you do that medicine dance.'

'You'll have your chance in six days,' Giselle promised. 'I do it every time the braves come in to draw their ammunition. We have to take the medicine off and put it back on again. And Ten Bears likes to see me do it.'

'He's not alone in that,' Waco declared, playing 'Matt Caxton' to the limit.

'Aren't you interested in how Emma comes to be here, Ed?' Giselle inquired, making it plain that she wanted the subject changing.

'I figure she'd tell me, was I to ask,' Dusty replied.

'Don't let my wife worry you, Edward,' Lampart said

soothingly. 'There not much to tell. We knew Emma from our theatre days and when I decided to open the saloon, I sent for her to come and run it. She agreed and has proved capable and efficient. There are no wanted posters out on her, or any murky secrets.'

'I never thought there was,' Dusty stated. 'But she's sure one hell of a woman, if you'll pardon the word, ma'am, and we get along just fine.'

'Lord!' Lampart barked, looking at the clock on the dining-room wall. 'Is that the time? I've got to go to a meeting of the Civic Council. Basmanov's trying to get the "no fires" rule cancelled again. Do you think it would be a good thing to let him, Ed?'

'Nope,' Dusty declared, aware of that answer being expected. 'You get all this town's smoke rising and somebody might figure out its here. Somebody we none of us want to see, like a cavalry patrol.'

'They're likely to be out in strength, seeing's one of their patrols got jumped,' the Kid went on. 'Maybe even strong enough to push through this far. Was I you, I'd stand firm against having fires during the day.'

'Rest assured that I will,' the mayor promised. 'I must go now.'

'We better drift down the barn, boys,' Dusty remarked. 'Time we've bedded the horses down, it'll be coming up towards dinner. Juanita and Red won't like it happen you pair's late to the Honest Man.'

CHAPTER THIRTEEN

IT'S OUR TOWN NOW, ED

'Nice neighbourly sort of folks hereabouts, Ed,' the Kid commented as the trio walked behind the street's buildings towards the livery barn. 'One or another of them, they've done just about every meanness 'cept hoss-stealing.'

'Bet some of them's even done that, but they're ashamed to admit it,' Waco went on. 'Not even their mothers could like 'em.'

'That's the way Lampart wants us to think,' Dusty admitted. 'Then we'll not be likely to throw in our hands with anybody else.'

'He made Emma out clean enough, though,' Waco remarked. 'You reckon it's the truth he told, Brother Ed?'

'I reckon so,' Dusty decided. 'He allows I've got a fond feeling for her and doesn't want to chance lying 'case I learn the truth.'

'He's one smart son-of-a-bitch,' drawled the Kid. 'Way he's played things, I can see how he's got Ten Bears and the medicine woman eating out of his hand.'

'We'll either have to bust up his medicine, or get rid of that ammunition before we pull out,' Dusty declared. 'Only, right now, I don't see how we're going to do either. So we'll keep playing along with him and watch our chance.'

'You reckon he trusts us all along the line now, Ed?' the Kid inquired.

'I'd say he's close to it,' Dusty replied. 'At least, he's letting us walk around without anybody hanging on to our shirt tails.'

When the trio reached the barn, they found it deserted except for Pigeons, the custodian of the town's winged messengers. Apparently Basmanov had already left to attend the meeting of the Civic Council. Being one of the Russian's supporters, Pigeons exhibited a distinct lack of cordiality and did not offer to help them with their work.

Having fed and done everything necessary for their horses' well-being, Dusty and his companions returned to the hotel. There they found Red and Juanita waiting, demanding the dinner treat which had been promised to them. Leaving the Kid and Waco to deal with the girls, Dusty went to his own room. Unlocking the door, he went in and slammed to a halt.

'What the hell—?' he growled, hurriedly closing the door.

Smiling at his surprise, Giselle rose from his bed. A long cloak was draped over a chair and Dusty could understand why she had worn it. All she had on was a most abbreviated white doeskin copy of an Indian girl's costume. In two pieces, it covered so little of her that its use on a stage would have resulted in the authorities closing down the theatre. Dusty had to admit that the brunette, small though she might be, had a body perfectly developed to complement the outfit. Looking at her, he could see that she had not been boasting when she claimed that she had held the Indian's attention while her husband had made his preparations to fool them.

'With Simmy at the Council meeting,' Giselle remarked, gliding towards Dusty in an undulating, sensual manner, 'I thought I'd come and show you my medicine dance costume.'

'You made a poor thought, ma'am,' Dusty answered, noticing that she halted well clear of his arms' reach.

'Don't you like me?' Giselle challenged, placing her hands on her head and rotating slowly to let him study her gorgeously moulded little body from all sides. 'I am beautiful, aren't I? Don't you think so?'

'You'll get no argument from me on that, ma'am,' Dusty admitted. 'Any man would, *Mrs*. Lampart.'

'But the fact that I am married bothers you.'

'What bothers me most is you're married to a man I admire and respect. Which being so, I reckon you'd best get covered over and head for home.'

'After I picked your lock to get in to see you?' Giselle pouted, but still kept her distance. 'You're sure that's what you want?'

'I've never been surer,' Dusty stated. 'I'm going to see the boys, ma'am, and I'd be truly grateful if you'll be gone when I get back.'

Leaving the room, Dusty shut the door. He went to his companions' quarters and found them getting ready, helped by the girls, for the evening's round of entertainment. With Red and Juanita present, he could not discuss Giselle's visit. When he returned to his room, he found that the brunette had gone.

That evening, on entering the saloon, Dusty went to where Lampart was sitting in solitary state at Emma's private table.

'I don't know whether to be riled or flattered,' the small Texan announced as he sat down.

'That went straight by me,' Lampart smiled.

'You sent your wife along to my room to try me out,' Dusty elaborated. 'That could've riled me up some, except that I reckoned you must trust me enough to know she'd be safe.'

'And you fully justified my faith in you,' the mayor praised, then the arrival of Youseman and le Blanc brought the conversation to an end.

During the evening, Dusty noticed an increased air of hostility between Basmanov's supporters and Lampart's clique. That told the small Texan why the mayor had been so loquacious at lunch and had sent Giselle to test his loyalty. Unless Dusty missed his guess, Lampart intended to lock horns with the Russian and settle who would control the town; so wanted to be sure of having 'Ed Caxton's' backing in the showdown.

Nothing was said on the subject until Emma mentioned it indirectly. It was after the saloon had closed for the night and she lay in bed with Dusty's arms around her.

'That was one stormy Council meeting this afternoon,

Ed,' the blonde remarked as they separated from a kiss.

'Was, huh?' Dusty replied, feeling her snuggling closer to him. 'Is Basmanov still pushing to get that "no fires" ruling changed?'

'That's only part of it,' Emma answered and kissed him with fiery passion. Drawing back her face, she went on, 'Mostly he's trying to make Simmy share out the Civic Improvement Fund instead of holding it all at his place.'

'Does Simmy do that?'

'He does. Even some of his own crowd aren't too happy about it.'

Having delivered the information, Emma started to make love. Dusty had never known her so insistent, or eager to give herself to him. After a time, they lay side by side on their backs and the blonde spoke again.

'I bet Simmy's got well over half a million dollars stashed away, Ed, what with the Fund, the profits from the saloon and his share in the other—'

'What other?' Dusty demanded as the words trailed off.

'Connolly and Youseman have found a way of embalming bodies so they'll keep long enough to be sent out of the Palo Duro and the bounty collected on them.'

'The hell you say!' Dusty growled, simulating surprise as he sat up and stared at the blonde through the darkness.

'It's true,' Emma insisted. 'That's why Youseman wasn't in the saloon the night you first came in. They were treating the bodies of those fellers you'd shot. I got the story from Youseman one night when he was drunk. What they do, I mean; it was before you got here. Him and Connolly found out how to do it at Simmy's suggestion. He fixed up the rest. Hatchet takes the bodies out to one of the towns where the sheriff's in cahoots with them. They had to take Basmanov in with them when he found out about it. None of them care much for that.'

'And nobody else knows?'

'Nobody. Youseman was so drunk that he's forgotten he told me. They put the bodies in trick coffins, so anybody who wants can see them. Then, when the lid's screwed on, the bottom opens to drop the corpse into the basement, the empty box is buried and the body sent out.'

'That's the sort of neat planning I'd expect from Simmy,' Dusty drawled.

'Is that all it means to you?' Emma asked, sitting up.

'What else should it mean?' Dusty countered.

'There's ten thousand dollars on each of your heads,' the blonde reminded him and slid closer to wrap her arms around him.

'Simmy's my friend,' Dusty pointed out.

'He was Ben Columbo's friend too,' Emma warned, sagging back to the pillow and drawing him with her. 'There's still an empty coffin in his grave.'

'Simmy needs me and the boys' guns,' Dusty began, being stopped by her lips crushing against his mouth and tongue slipping between his teeth.

'The time will come when he doesn't,' the blonde cautioned at the completion of the kiss. Her hands roamed over Dusty's body. 'What a waste it would be, Ed. Embalming you, I mean.'

'I'll have something to say afore they get the chance to do it,' Dusty threatened.

'So will I,' Emma promised and pressed her lips lightly to his. Then she whispered, 'Ed. Over half a million is a lot of money.'

There the matter came to an end. Clearly waiting for Dusty to make a comment, Emma said no more. He made no response, other than returning her caresses, until sleep claimed them both. The exertions of their love-making caused them to be late out of bed next morning. In fact, it was way past noon before they had eaten breakfast and dressed to go downstairs. They found Waco and the Kid in the bar room, although Red and Juanita were no longer in evidence.

'You pair expecting a war?' Dusty inquired, nodding to the Winchester in the Kid's right hand.

'Nope,' Waco replied. 'Last night my Red gal got saying how she just loves turkey. So Comanch's fixing to go out and shoot one for her.'

'There's a gentleman for you,' Emma praised. 'The boys take after you, Ed.'

'They couldn't pick a better ex—' Dusty began, then

stopped to stare as the side door opened and Giselle ran in. 'What's up, Mrs. Lampart?'

'It's Basmanov,' the brunette replied. She was wearing her usual style of clothing and looked concerned. 'He's lit the fire in his office stove and Simmy's going down there to make him put it out.'

'Could be he'll need help,' Dusty barked. 'Let's go, boys.'

'I'll see to Mrs. Lampart,' Emma remarked, catching hold of the brunette's right arm in a firm rather than gentle grip. 'Leave her to me, Ed.'

'*Gracias, querida,*' Dusty drawled. 'Don't you fret none, ma'am, we'll see Simmy comes back safe.'

Giselle had obviously wasted no time in bringing the news. Leaving the saloon by the rear door, the three Texans saw Lampart half-way along the back of Doctor Connolly's premises. Hearing their footsteps, he turned to face them.

'What – How—?' the mayor gasped, showing surprise and relief.

'Your lady told us what's happening,' Dusty explained. 'We concluded that you'd need some help.'

'I do,' Lampart admitted and indicated the white-handled revolver thrust into his waistband. 'After the way Basmanov took on at yesterday's meeting, I'm sure this is his way of calling me out for a showdown.'

'He'll have friends along,' Dusty declared, not offering to walk on.

'It's possible,' the mayor admitted. 'Pigeons will be there. Probably Diebitch, the blacksmith, Rossi, his usual clique.'

'Then we're going to play it smart,' Dusty decided. 'I don't reckon they've seen us yet. So you and me'll go along the street, bold as all get out, right through the front door.'

'Just the two of us?'

'Matt and Comanch'll be around when we need them.'

Leaving his companions, Dusty accompanied the mayor at a leisurely pace through an alley to the street. Already the smoke rising from the barn's chimney had attracted considerable attention. Men and women pointed it out to each other. Then they turned their gaze to Dusty and Lampart. Only le Blanc offered to help. Carrying a twin-barrelled shotgun, he ran from his shop.

'It's come then, Simmy?' the barber greeted.

'As you say, Jean,' Lampart confirmed. 'It's come.'

'Don't walk so fast,' Dusty advised. 'Diebitch's watching us from the front door, so we'll be expected. Leave them sweat it out a whiles – And let my boys get into place before we go in.'

'I don't see Matt or Comanche,' Lampart reported worriedly, glancing in passing along the alley which separated the barn from its next-door neighbour.

'It's lucky Diebitch's ducked back in,' Dusty growled. 'You'd've give the whole snap away. They're around. You can count on it.'

Walking on, the three men stepped through the open front doors of the barn. With le Blanc to his left and Lampart at the right, Dusty studied his surroundings. Basmanov and the slim, vicious-looking Diebitch confronted the trio, but there was no sign of any other members of the Russian's faction.

'You know the penalty for lighting a fire between dawn and sundown, Ivan?' Lampart challenged.

'I do,' Basmanov admitted. 'And you'll pay it. You and one of your magic tricks lit the stove.'

'Now who'll believe that?' Lampart asked.

'I reckon they'll believe whichever of us comes out of it alive,' Basmanov grinned. 'Only you wouldn't have the guts to face me man to man.'

'Wouldn't I?' countered Lampart.

'You've brought le Blanc and Caxton along,' the Russian pointed out.

'Only to see fair doings,' Dusty drawled. 'If Mr. Diebitch'll back off, me and Jean'll leave you gents settle this between you.'

'That suits me,' Diebitch stated fervently and moved aside.

'And me,' Lampart declared. 'Go and wait by the doors, gentlemen.'

'To show I don't want no edge,' Basmanov said, when

Dusty and le Blanc had obeyed. 'I'll ask you to count to five, Mr. Caxton. We'll draw when you get there.'

'Go ahead, Ed,' Lampart commanded.

'One!' Dusty said. 'Two!'

Down drove Basmanov's right hand, closing about the butt of his gun. At the same moment, he saw a mocking smile playing on Lampart's lips. It was the expression of a man who had out-bluffed a bluffer.

As soon as Basmanov moved, the mayor whipped out his own revolver. Although it had an ivory handle, it proved to be a snub-nosed British Webley Bulldog and not the Colt Peacemaker from the top of his desk. Twice the weapon crashed, with a speed that was only possible by trigger pressure – as opposed to fanning the hammer – when using a self-cocking, double-action mechanism. Although he had started his draw slightly after the Russian, Lampart had about six inches less barrel to get clear. That made all the difference. His bullets tore into Basmanov's chest before the other's gun could point at him.

'Get them!' Diebitch screamed, grabbing for the revolver he wore.

Throwing up his shotgun, le Blanc cut loose from waist level. Seven of the nine buckshot balls which belched from the right hand tube found their mark and flung Diebitch lifeless from his feet.

While Dusty had agreed to take a passive role, he had been under no delusions regarding Basmanov's sense of fair play. So he had been prepared for treachery and knew instinctively where it would come from. Sure enough, Pigeons loomed into sight from behind the hay-bales at the front of the loft and started to swing a shotgun to his shoulder. Even as Lampart's Webley spoke, Dusty's hands crossed with their usual speed. The small Texan took the extra split-second needed to raise his right hand weapon to eye-level and take aim. He shot the only way he dared in the circumstances, for an instant kill. Passing Pigeons' rising shotgun, the .45 bullet winged into his head.

Big and bulky, the blacksmith had also risen from concealment in the loft. The ambush had been planned. That was obvious from the way the man took aim at and shot le Blanc, although he did so too late to save Diebitch. In echo to the blacksmith's revolver, Dusty's left hand Colt lined and barked. Hit in the body, Pigeons' companion screamed, spun around, toppled over the bales and crashed to the floor below.

In the tack-room, Rossi and another man gripped their revolvers and waited to cut in on the fight which would determine who ran Hell. So interested were they in what was going on between Basmanov and Lampart that they failed to notice the face which peered in through the window. On seeing the Russian's bid fail, Rossi prepared to throw open the door leading into the stable.

Having reached the barn undetected, Waco saw enough through the window to know that he must act fast. Kicking open the outside door as he had learned to do from Dusty, he plunged into the tack-room. The two men heard the crash and spun around with their weapons thrusting in the youngster's direction. Left, right, left, right, flame erupted from the muzzles of Waco's Army Colts. Rossi died instantly, a bullet severing his jugular vein. Hit in the shoulder, the second man dropped his gun and stumbled into the stable. Being unarmed did not save him. Turning fast, Lampart shot him in the head.

While that was happening, the Kid raced in through the back doors. Bounding along the gap between two lots of stalls, he appeared before another pair of Basmanov's supporters as they came from one of the storerooms. Seeing the dark-faced savage, they forgot their intention of shooting Lampart and tried to turn their guns on the Kid. Lead hissed by him, calling for an immediate response. Working his Winchester's lever at its fastest possible speed, he poured out eight bullets in an arc that encompassed the two men's torsos. Both went down, torn to doll-rags by the tempest of flying lead.

No more men appeared. The bloody battle for mastery of the town had come to an end. Horses squealed, snorted, reared and kicked at their stalls in fright as the acrid powder smoke wafted away.

'See to the horses – Comanch', Matt,' Dusty ordered,

having to make an effort to prevent himself using their real names. Looking at le Blanc, he went on, 'Jean's cashed in.'

'He's been avenged,' Lampart answered and started to go around Basmanov's party to check on their condition. 'And he'll have plenty of company; they're all dead too.'

People came pouring into the barn. Outlaws went to help the Kid and Waco calm down the horses. Townsmen studied the bodies and exchanged glances. Those who had supported Lampart showed their satisfaction. On other faces, anxiety and concern left their marks. Those were the emotions of Basmanov's less active partisans, who wondered what the future held for them on account of it. Already the fencesitters were beaming their approval at the mayor. However, Lampart ignored all of them. After ordering the jeweller to put out the fire in the office's stove and directing Youseman to give le Blanc the best possible funeral, he apologized to such outlaws as were present for disturbing their horses. Then he called the three Texans to him, thanked them for their support and asked them to accompany him to his home.

On the street, the men found Giselle, Red, Juanita and Emma waiting. The blonde held a bottle of champagne and declared that the victory called for a celebration. Giving his agreement, Lampart took them to his house and established them comfortably in the sitting-room. With the drinks served and toasts to their continued success drunk, Dusty decided to obtain some information.

'How did you know when to set the fire off, Simmy?' the small Texan asked. 'If you'd done it too early, we might none of us been around to back your play.'

'I waited until I saw Comanche and Matt taking the young ladies back to the saloon. Emma's maid had already drawn the curtains in her bedroom, which meant you and she were up and about. So I made my arrangements, knowing your brother and Comanche would be waiting for you.'

'How'd you get in and light the fire?' Waco inquired. 'You couldn't've just touched her off and got out, somebody'd likely've seen you.'

'It's a trick I learned, making a fire start at a given

moment. I won't say more than that, a magician is under oath not to divulge the nature of his secrets. I went there, picked the office because it was empty, made my arrangements and came back to await results.'

'You knew Basmanov'd see the smoke and guess what your game was,' Dusty drawled. 'But you counted on him wanting a showdown, gathering his stoutest side-kicks and waiting for you to come.'

'That's true,' Lampart admitted. 'I also knew that, with you helping me, I had the edge. None of them could even come close to matching your gun skill.'

'That's for sure,' Waco put in. 'They didn't have the sense to watch the outside windows.'

'All went off perfectly,' Lampart declared, showing no hint of regret over le Blanc's death. 'It's my town now.'

'*Your* town, Simmy?' Dusty queried, seeing Emma throw him a glance pregnant with meaning.

'That wasn't what I meant,' Lampart amended. 'It's *our* town now, Ed.'

'I said you could count on Simmy to do the right thing, Ed,' Emma remarked.

CHAPTER FOURTEEN

TAKE YOUR CLAWS OFF MY MAN

In all his eventful young life, Dusty Fog had never received a shock to equal that which greeted him as he entered the mayor's office towards sundown on the day after the gun battle. Fortunately, Lampart had his back to the door and did not see the small Texan's reaction to the sight of the woman who was placing a bulky set of saddlebags into one of the deposit boxes. Straightening up and closing the lid, she stared in Dusty's direction. At first surprise played on her strikingly beautiful features, to be replaced almost immediately by an expression which denoted understanding.

Black hair flowed from beneath the brim of a grey Stetson hat with a band decorated by silver conchas. She wore a fringed buckskin jacket, open down its front to exhibit a dark grey shirt tucked into figure-hugging black riding breeches. High-heeled boots with spurs attached graced her feet. The clothes served to display a body every bit as voluptuously curvaceous as Emma Nene's. Emphasizing the full contours of her hips, a gunbelt slanted down with the tip of the holster tied to her magnificently moulded right thigh. In the holster, carefully positioned to facilitate a fast draw, rode what looked like a wooden-handled Colt Model 1851 Navy revolver.

Without the need for closer examination, Dusty knew the woman's gun to be a five shot copy of the Navy Colt manufactured by the now-defunct Manhattan Firearms Company. Going by her display of emotion on his arrival, she could identify him despite his clothes, the beard and moustache. She had been a blonde on their two previous meetings, but Dusty found no difficulty in recognizing the famous lady outlaw, Belle Starr.

'Ed!' Belle greeted, her voice a pleasant, warmly-inviting Southern drawl. 'I just might have known I'd find you here, after all the things I've been reading about you-all in the *Texas State Gazette*.'

'You know each other?' Lampart inquired, bringing his gaze from its contemplation of Belle's physique.

There was a hint of suspicion in the mayor's voice and Dusty could figure out what had caused it. Lampart had not forgotten how 'Ed Caxton' had claimed to have led a law-abiding life, until committing the robbery which had resulted in him fleeing for safety to Hell. So Lampart was wondering how he could have made the acquaintance of such a prominent member of outlaw society.

'Why sure,' Dusty agreed, thinking fast. 'It was while we were with the Army up in the Indian Nations. Me and the boys got sent with a patrol to search for Miss Belle at her pappy's place.'

'Why they just did me the biggest favour in my whole life,' Belle went on. 'The three of them were sent to search the barn and Comanche found my hiding place. But Ed said for me to be covered up again and they never let on where I was to that mean old officer.'

In view of her close relationship with Mark Counter,[*] Dusty had not expected Belle to betray him. She had recognized him immediately, recollected the story of the robbery in the newspapers and guessed what was happening. No matter why she had come to Hell, it seemed that she was willing to play along with the small Texan's game.

'You paid us back in Dallas,' Dusty pointed out, feeling that so short an acquaintance would not account for her recognizing him. 'If you hadn't loaned me that five hundred dollars, I might've had to kill some of the gambling

---

[*] How that relationship began, developed and finally ended is told in the 'The Bounty On Belle Starr's Scalp' episode of *Troubled Range, The Bad Bunch, Rangeland Hercules*, the 'A Lady Known as Belle' episode of *The Hard Riders* and *Guns in the Night*.

man's side-kicks to stop them pestering me for it.'

'I had my money's worth,' Belle claimed, darting an arch smile at Lampart. She too felt that the situation needed a little expanding. 'Ed's quite a man, you know, Simmy. Although I don't suppose you *could* know, not that way.'

'I suppose not,' Lampart agreed stiffly and looked at Dusty, 'Miss Starr—'

'I've already said you can call me "Belle",' the girl interrupted.

'Belle has just arrived, Ed,' the mayor went on. 'I've explained the rules of the town and she agrees to them.'

'That figures,' Dusty drawled, glancing at the girl's gun-belt. 'Did you have trouble getting here, Belle?'

'None. But I was just a teensy mite worried when the guide said I'd have to hand over my guns. He was telling the truth about me getting them back after I'd talked to the mayor.'

'Why'd you need to come?' Dusty challenged, knowing some such comment would be expected by Lampart.

'Belle had heard of our community,' the mayor injected, just a shade too quickly. 'And, with the Indian Nations being somewhat disturbed—'

'*Disturbed!*' Belle ejaculated. 'Land-sakes a-mercy, Ed, it's hotter than a two dollar pistol up there right now. So I concluded I'd better stay away from home for a spell. Of course I'd heard of Hell and decided to take a look at it.'

'Seeing's how Belle's such an old friend of mine,' Dusty remarked to the mayor, 'I reckon we can forget her contribution to the Civic Improvement Fund.'

'Well, I admit a twentieth of my money does seem a lot,' Belle purred, glancing at the stack of bills which lay alongside the white-handled Peacemaker on the desk. 'But I shouldn't have any special favours. It just wouldn't be fitting, Ed.'.

'A *twentieth's* a whole heap of money,' Dusty said coldly. 'Has Simmy introduced you to his wife, Belle?'

'I was going to, after we'd concluded our business,' the mayor declared, with an annoyed glare at the small Texan.

'If she's busy, it can wait her convenience, Simmy,'

Belle smiled. 'Why don't you show me to the hotel, Ed. I'm just dying to hear all about that robbery you and the boys pulled.'

Although he threw a scowl at Dusty, Lampart raised no objections. Belle locked her box and dropped the keys into a jacket pocket. Then she and Dusty left the office. Giselle peered around the curtain at the back end of the hall, but withdrew without coming to be introduced. On emerging from the mayor's house, Dusty became aware of somebody watching him. Looking at the saloon, he saw two of the girls standing on the first floor's verandah. They were displaying considerable interest in Belle and himself. Even as he watched, one of them darted into the building. Dusty did not need much thought to figure out where she was going. So he concluded that he had better get Belle off the street before Emma came to investigate.

'What's the game, Dusty?' Belle asked as he started her moving away from the saloon. 'I nearly had a fit when you walked in. Luckily I remembered that story in the paper and came up with the right answer – or some of it.'

'Thanks for not saying who I am,' Dusty replied. 'I hoped you wouldn't.'

'Now play fair with me,' Belle suggested. 'I'm here on business and I'd like to know where I—'

'Mr. Caxton,' called a voice and Dusty saw the jeweller waddling across the street in his direction. 'I was hoping to see you. I've had the clasp on that necklance repaired and it's ready for you.'

'*Gracias,*' Dusty answered. 'I'll come around later and—'

'Now who would you be buying a necklace for, Ed?' Belle challenged, a merry gleam dancing in her eyes. 'Come on. I'm dying to see it.'

'Maybe you should go and get a room at the hotel,' Dusty told her.

'There's time for that later,' Belle insisted. 'Come on.'

So far, Dusty observed as he made for the jeweller's shop, Emma had not made an appearance. The delay would allow her time to do so before he could get Belle inside the hotel. So, in the interests of peace and quiet, he figured he had best take the lady outlaw out of the blonde's sight. They entered the shop without Emma having emerged from the Honest Man. Passing around the end of the counter, the owner disappeared into a back room. He seemed to take an exceptionally long time before he returned carrying a magnificent diamond necklace. Dusty could hear significant sounds from the street, but hoped he might be wrong about their meaning. From what he could see through the window, he doubted if he was.

'My!' Belle breathed, laying a hand on Dusty's sleeve. 'Now isn't that the sweetest lil ole trinket you ever did see?'

The front door flew open and a furious feminine voice hissed, 'Take your claws off my man!'

Turning with the speed of a wildcat preparing to defend itself, Belle confronted Emma. The blonde was dressed ready for her night's work and a couple of rings with sizeable stones flashed on her fingers. Ignoring the people who gathered behind her, Emma looked Belle over from head to toe. The saloongirls had spread the word and a number of men and women waited to see what would develop.

'Easy, Emma,' Dusty said soothingly. 'I was just taking Miss Starr down to the hotel.'

'Why, Ed,' Belle purred. 'You've never called me "Miss Starr" before.'

Annoyance bit at Dusty. Instead of Belle letting him handle things, she seemed set on provoking trouble. Dull red flooded into Emma's cheeks and she bunched her right hand to form a capable-looking fist.

'He won't do it ag—!' the blonde began, drawing back her arm.

Out flashed Belle's Manhattan, its hammer clicking back and muzzle pointing at Emma's heaving bosom. Poised to attack, the protruding stone of a ring glinting evilly on her clenched fist, the blonde stood very still.

'You try to ram that blazer into my face,' Belle threatened, 'and I'll put a window in your apples.'

'I can soon enough take the rings off!' Emma spat back, making a move as if to do so.

'Please ladies,' the jeweller implored. 'No fighting in here.'

'Let it drop, both of you!' Dusty ordered.

'If *you* say so, Ed,' Belle replied. 'What do folks do for entertainment around here, Mr. Jewellery-Man?'

'G – Go to the Honest Man Saloon,' the shop's owner replied.

'You put your face inside it,' Emma promised grimly, 'and I'll throw you right back out.'

'Will you be there tonight, Ed?' Belle inquired.

'That won't matter to you,' Emma declared before Dusty could reply. 'What I said goes. If you show your face in my place tonight, gun or no gun, I'll make you wish you'd hid in some other brothel instead of coming here.'

'That's big talk for a fat old harridan,' Belle jeered, conscious that the exchange had an audience. 'I'll be there tonight. Without my gun and, to give you a chance, wearing moccasins. That'll make us even, for all your blazers and long talons.'

With that, Belle holstered the Manhattan and pushed by Emma to leave the building. For a moment, the blonde appeared to be on the verge of hurling herself after the lady outlaw. Then, glancing at her rings and finger-nails, Emma stalked out of the door. She did not even look at Dusty before departing.

'Whoo!' ejaculated the jeweller and ran the tip of his tongue across his lips. 'It should be something to see at the Honest Man tonight, Mr. Caxton.'

'Likely,' Dusty admitted absently, wondering why Belle had taken such an attitude.

'How about the necklace?' the man asked as Dusty turned from the counter.

'I reckon I'd best take it with me,' the small Texan decided, thinking that it might prove useful as a peace offering to Emma.

Apparently practically everybody in town shared the jeweller's summation. Dusty had never seen such a crowd as he found in the Honest Man Saloon on his arrival at nine o'clock. There were people present he would never have expected to find in a saloon. Giselle sat with Lampart

148

at Emma's table. Other townsmen had also brought their wives. The madam of the brothel was there, accompanied by her whole staff. So far, neither Emma nor Belle had made an appearance. Dusty figured that they soon would.

Despite his efforts, Dusty had failed to change either of their minds. Although delighted with the necklace, Emma had stated the only way she would forget the incident was if Belle made a public apology and never entered the saloon. Due to the interest her arrival had aroused, Dusty could not manage to get Belle alone for more than a few seconds. Asked to let the matter drop, she had declared herself willing to do so; if Emma invited her into the Honest Man.

Consulting the Kid and Waco, Dusty had finally decided to leave the women to settle the issue themselves. From what Mark had told them, Belle could take care of herself. She had also fixed it so that Emma would be unable to wear the dangerous rings and most likely had to cut short her nails. So both should escape serious damage. Waco had warned that the town would deeply resent any interference which halted the fight. Already, the trio suspected, Lampart was seeking a way to remove them. There was no point in giving him a weapon with which to turn the population against them.

'Mig Santiago will be annoyed to have missed this,' Giselle remarked, after Dusty had sat down and exchanged greetings.

Any comment the small Texan might have considered making on the subject of the Mexican's departure, under pressure from his financially-embarrassed gang, went unsaid. The low hum of conversation died away around the room. Every head swung to stare at Belle as she strolled through the batwing doors.

True to her promise, the lady outlaw had left off her gunbelt and boots. Missing too were the Stetson and her jacket. She made an atrractive picture in her moccasins, riding breeches as tight as a second skin, shirt with its sleeves rolled up and hands covered by thin black leather gloves.

Posted to keep watch for Belle, a girl on the balcony

darted away. When Emma came slinking gracefully down the stairs, the way in which she was clothed threatened to overshadow the black-haired beauty's appearance. The blonde wore nothing but a brief, lace-trimmed white bodice, black silk tights and high heeled slippers with pompons on the toes. Showing her unadorned hands, she drew on a pair of white gloves. Then, in a silence that could almost be felt, she advanced to the centre of the area in front of the bar which had been cleared of tables and chairs to make room for the anticipated battle.

'I'll set up drinks all round after I've handed her her needings, folks,' Belle announced, moving towards Emma like a great cat stalking its prey.

'*If* she licks me,' the blonde countered. 'I'll give drinks to the house all night.'

That was all the conversation carried out. Warily the two gorgeous creatures circled each other. Suddenly Belle whipped her arm right back and swung her open palm in a round-house slap to Emma's left cheek. It cracked with a sharp, vicious sound, snapping the blonde's head around and bringing an involuntary squeak of pain. For all that, Emma responded almost immediately by whipping out first one hand, then the other. The explosive smacks of her palms against Belle's face rang out loud. Eager to follow up her advantage, the blonde crowded forward with arms flailing. Bewildered by the onslaught, Belle was forced to retreat. Excited yells rose from the crowd. Men and women came to their feet, moving to form a wall of humanity around the open space in which the girls were tangling.

Desperate to halt the stinging punishment, Belle suddenly entwined her fingers into Emma's blonde tresses. She backed off a long stride, hauling the saloonkeeper's head down and throwing up her knee. An experienced bar room brawler, Emma had known what to expect. Swiftly she folded her arms in front of her face and Belle's knee struck them. Although the blonde had saved herself from serious damage, the impact snapped her erect. Belle had retained her hold on Emma's hair, so the pain caused by the halting of her head's upwards movement ripped into the blonde. Letting out a screech, Emma sank both hands deep into Belle's free-flowing black hair. She jerked and twisted at the ensnared locks with deliberate fury, only to have Belle reply in a similar manner.

Lurching from side to side, their heads bobbing and shaking with the violence they put into the hair-yanking, the girls also staggered back and forwards a few steps at a time. They clung determinedly to each other's hair, looking as if they desired to hand-scalp each other. Forehead to forehead, they panted and grunted, striving all the time to retain their balance on wide spread legs.

It could not last. With a final wrench bringing squeaks of agony, almost as if by mutual consent, they jerked free their hands and went into a clinch. For a few seconds they tussled on their feet. Then Belle managed to twist away and drag Emma over her buttocks. Turning a somersault, the blonde went to the floor. However, she had clung on to Belle and the outlaw followed her. Curling over in mid-air, Belle lit down on her back.

Rolling over swiftly, Emma writhed until her open thighs made an arch over Belle's head and her knees held the outlaw's arms pinned to the floor. Bending forward, the blonde thrust her fingers on to the trapped girl's bust. With the pain knifing into her, Belle supported herself on her bent left leg, and, lifting her rump from the unyielding planks, jerked her right knee hard against the top of the blonde's forward tilted skull. The blow caused Emma to remove her fingers from the sensitive region and lurch away.

Snatching her arms from beneath Emma's knees, Belle rolled into a sitting position. She turned just in time to meet the blonde's diving attack. Bust to bust, fingers again ripping at hair, they pitched full length on the floor. Belle's legs were doubled under her, but she managed to writhe them free. A sudden heave brought the outlaw on top, both hands tugging outwards at hanks of blonde hair. Shrieking in torment, Emma tried to bow her body upwards. Her left hand lost its grip on Belle's hair. Scrabbling for a fresh hold, she grasped the open neck of Belle's shirt. A fresh surge of pain from the tortured locks of hair caused Emma to wrench savagely at the garment. Buttons popped and, dragged out of Belle's breeches, the shirt split open down its front.

Angered by the damage to her clothing, Belle released the hair. Wriggling until her right knee rammed against Emma's abdomen, she sought for revenge. Drawn down around her right bicep, the shirt did not entangle her arms sufficiently to inconvenience her. Laying her right hand on Emma's face, she pressed the blonde's head to the floor. Greedily the outlaw's left fist clamped on the front of the bodice, tugging and pulling until the flimsy material came apart from décolleté to waist.

Almost unseated by Emma's furious struggles, Belle advanced to sit astride her shoulders. Transferring her hand to the side of the blonde's head, she drew back the other fist ready to pound Emma's face. At the table, Dusty wondered if he should intervene. To do so might bring about his death, for the wildly excited crowd would expect to see the fight through to a decisive victory for one or the other girl. Yet, held down in such a way, Emma might suffer serious damage at the hands of her enraged rival. Before he could reach a decision, Dusty saw Emma was shouting something. Although the noisy acclaim of the spectators prevented the small Texan from catching the words, Belle obviously heard them.

Instead of pummelling the blonde's face to a bloody ruin, the outlaw's fist held back. Like a flash, Emma braced her feet and head against the floor. Up curved her body, with a force that flung Belle forward and away from her. Rolling on to her stomach as Belle landed face down, Emma plunged on to the outlaw's back. For several seconds, the blonde remained on top. With her thighs squirming to hold down Belle's legs, the blonde hooked her left arm under and around the other's throat while her right alternately punched the trapped head and tore away the remains of the shirt.

Screeching and struggling with the strength of rage-filled desperation, Belle contrived to roll on to her right side. The arm was still about her neck and the blonde's legs, the knees showing whitely through the ruptured silk of the tights, straddled her hips. While Belle's right arm attempted to drag Emma away by the hair, her left fingers raked ineffectively at the blonde's ribs to complete the destruction and removal of the bodice.

Oblivious of her naked torso, Emma fought on. So did Belle. Losing her choke-hold, the blonde allowed the outlaw to reach a sitting position. Then, sitting up herself, she wrapped her legs in a scissor grip about Belle's bare mid-section. Gasping as the crushing pressure bit at her, Belle clawed at Emma's upper leg in a futile effort at escaping. Tilting sideways and resting on her left elbow, the saloon-keeper slammed her clenched right hand into the centre of the outlaw's face. Blood trickled from Belle's nostrils. Mouthing croaks of pain, Belle took her hands from Emma's right leg. She put them to better use by grabbing hold of and crushing at the blonde's jutting bare right breast. Emma's scream rang out loud. Lifting her right leg, she shoved up with the left to try to dislodge her tormentress. Such was Belle's relief at the end of the scissors that she released her own hold and rolled away.

Dragging themselves to their feet, the girls stood for a moment to regain something of their energy. Then they rushed at each other with fists flying. Wildly propelled knuckles impacted on faces, busts, stomachs, or missed as chance dictated. Coming in close to try to minimize the punishment being inflicted, they went into a mindless tangle of primitive, unscientific wrestling. Arms, legs, elbows, hands and feet were used indiscriminately and teeth brought into play. Emma was bare-footed, her tights in ribbons, while Belle had lost one moccasin and her other leg showed where the breeches' seam had split. Six times they made their feet and went down, while the crowds screamed itself hoarse, encouraging them to further efforts.

On the seventh time of rising, the girls clutched at one another's throats and held on with a choking grip. Reddish blotches showed around their fingers as the digits gouged into sweat-soddened flesh. Guttural sounds broke from them. Although fairly evenly matched, Emma had a slight weight advantage. Not much, but enough in their present condition. Slowly she bore Belle backwards, but without causing the other to let go.

In an attempt to free herself, Belle slid her legs between Emma's spread-apart feet and lowered her rump to the floor. And found she had made a serious mistake. She was sitting with the back almost touching the dais on which, at other times, the band played. Before she could rectify the situation, Belle was trapped. Spreading open her thighs, Emma lunged to kneel on the dais and crush Belle against it.

Realizing the consequences of failure, Belle put all her strength into a desperate effort. Bracing her shoulders against the dais, she thrust forward. Finding herself being tilted off balance, the blonde tried to spring to the rear. Landing awkwardly, she sat down hard. Lurching upright, Belle swung around her right leg. The sole of the bare foot slammed against the side of Emma's jaw. As she fell backwards, Belle stumbled away.

Sobbing with exhaustion, the outlaw turned to defend herself. She saw Emma lying supine, right leg bent, right hand clasped on her forehead and left arm stretched out limply. Calling on her last dregs of energy, Belle returned to the blonde's side. Standing astride the motionless figure, Belle folded her legs until her rump came to rest on Emma's bosom. She had the blonde at her mercy, arms trapped beneath her knees, but waited to regather her strength. Then she felt two hands beneath her arm-pits, lifting her. For a moment, she tried to struggle and twisted her head to see who was holding her.

'For God's sake, Belle,' Dusty Fog said, dragging her from the unconscious blonde. 'Leave Emma be. She's licked.'

'T-Take-me-hotel!' Belle croaked back. 'D-Damn it. Take me. I've won and it's due to me.'

CHAPTER FIFTEEN

WE HAD TO KNOW WHO'S BOSS

'I hope you haven't got the wrong idea, Dusty,' Belle Starr remarked as she stood with her back to him and, wincing a little, donned a flimsy nightgown. 'Because only one man has ever shared my bed.'

'So Mark told me,' Dusty replied. 'What the hell did you fight Emma for?'

As soon as Dusty had seen Emma was beaten, he had left the table and prevented Belle from inflicting further punishment. Nobody had objected, being more concerned with reaping the full benefits of the blonde's defeat. Deeply puzzled by the lady outlaw's behaviour, he had escorted her to the hotel. She had clearly made arrangements for her return. A hip bath, filled with warm water, stood in the corner of her room and she had used it to wash away the dirt, sawdust and sweat of the fight. Powdered witch-hazel leaves had stopped the bleeding from her nose and other minor abrasions. Although she had a mouse under her left eye and a mottling of bruises, she did not appear to have suffered any serious damage.

'For two reasons,' Belle said, sitting on the edge of the bed. 'I don't take to blonde calico-cats mean-mouthing me. And I wanted a chance for a long, private talk with you.' She gingerly touched her swollen, discoloured left eye. 'If I'd known how tough that girl of yours was, I'd've picked an easier way of doing it.'

'She's not my gal,' Dusty corrected. 'Except that she figures "Ed Caxton" might be able to help her against Mayor Lampart.'

'Does she?' Belle said, with some interest. 'And why is "Ed Caxton" here?'

'I could ask you the same thing. Day comes when the Indian Nations gets so "disturbed" Belle Starr has to run out, I'll start voting Republican.'

'Considering what I went through tonight, just to be all on our lonesome with you, *Ed* honey, I think *you* should answer me first.'

'All right,' Dusty drawled, not offering to leave the chair he had occupied since entering the room. 'Me and the boys came here to find out all we could about this town, so that the Governor can figure out a way to close it down.'

'I thought that's about what it would be,' Belle admitted. 'From all I've heard, you've been busy since you got here. Word has it that you're Lampart's right hand gun.'

'I've made myself useful,' Dusty said, with an expression of distaste. 'So far, everybody I've had to kill've been fellers who deserved it.'

'You're going to break Lampart before you leave,' Belle commented, as a statement and not a question.

'If I can,' Dusty agreed and told her all he had learned since coming to Hell.

Belle sat and listened without interruption all through Dusty's lengthy recital of the town's history. Relying on Mark Counter's assessment of her character, the small Texan held back no aspect of the citizens' and the mayor's infamy. Revulsion flickered on her bruised features as she heard of how men had been murdered for the bounty on their heads. Then he mentioned one last thing; an item which he figured would seal her hatred of Lampart.

'Lordy lord!' the lady outlaw ejaculated. 'You mean he's actually given repeaters and ammunition to the *Kweharehnuh*?'

'I wouldn't lie to you, Belle,' Dusty declared.

'Lands-sakes-a-mercy!' the girl gasped, shutting her eyes and visualizing what could result from the mayor's actions. 'They're a prime set of scum, the people here. But I do declare that Lampart's the worst of them all.'

'Out and away the worst,' Dusty confirmed.

'I'm right pleased that I was asked to come here and help rob him,' Belle announced.

Almost ten seconds ticked by before Dusty spoke. From along the street came the sounds of celebration. If the noise was anything to go by, the crowd were enjoying to the full the free liquor brought to them by Belle's victory over Emma.

'So that's why you're here,' Dusty breathed. 'Who sent for you?'

'I didn't have time to find out before your sweet-honey called me for a showdown,' Belle replied, a faint smile playing on her lips.

'You don't know?'

'I had this offer, through a man I can trust, to come here for the job. I was given a thousand dollars travelling money and half a hundred dollar bill. Whoever wanted me here would show me the other half and we could make our deal. It seemed worth looking into, so I came along. I'd heard about having to hand over a tenth of the loot, so I fetched along around fifteen thousand dollars.'

'That's a heap of cash money—'

'I'm not a two-bit thief,' Belle pointed out. 'So I'd be expected to have plenty. Anyways, all but three thousand of it's Confederate States' currency. And I did get a reduction from Simmy.'

'So I noticed,' Dusty grinned. 'Mark always said you could charm a bird down off a tree, had you a mind to.'

'It saves waving a gun ar—' Belle began.

'What's up?' Dusty whispered as the girl stopped speaking and adopted an attitude of listening.

'Somebody's just come and's listening outside the door!' Belle answered, just as quietly. 'Quick. Strip to the waist, Stay sat and lift your legs so's I can pull your boots off.'

Swiftly, Dusty unbuckled and removed his gunbelt. Then, while Belle drew off first one boot and the other, he divested himself of tie, shirt and undershirt. Having completed her part of the undressing, Belle rose, threw back the covers and climbed into bed. Drawing his right hand Colt, Dusty tip-toed across the room. Looking at what should have been a continuous strip of lamplight glowing

157

between the floor and the bottom of the door, he made out the dark blobs caused by the listener's feet. Turning the key, he unlocked and threw open the door in practically one motion.

'What the—?' Dusty spat out as a figure clad in a hooded cape almost fell through the door into his arms.

'Let me in, Ed!' Emma Nene begged, *sotto voce* but urgently. 'Quick. I'm not here to make trouble.'

Having already seen the thing she gripped in her right hand, Dusty knew that the blonde was speaking the truth. So he withdrew and allowed her to dart by. Glancing along the lamp-illuminated passage to make sure they had not been observed, Dusty closed and relocked the door.

'I didn't think you could make it before morning, after the licking I handed you,' Belle smiled, sitting up and swinging her legs from the bed. 'Do you have the other half of the bill?'

Thrusting back the hood, Emma allowed her cloak to fall open. Under it, she wore the nightgown which Dusty had come to know so well during his stay in Hell. Like Belle, the blonde had bathed and attended to her injuries. Emma's top lip was swollen and her right eye resembled a Blue Point oyster peeping out of its shell. Walking to the bed as if Dusty did not exist, she held out the half of a hundred dollar bill which had told him that she had come on a peaceful visit. It had also given him food for speculation, in view of what Belle had said.

'Here's mine,' the blonde said. 'Where's yours?'

Taking down her gunbelt, from where it hung around the post at the head of the bed, Belle produced the other half of the bill from a secret pocket. She handed it to Dusty and told Emma to do the same.

'They match,' the small Texan affirmed, placing the edges together. 'Now will somebody tell me what the hell it's all about?'

'Your sweet-honey had me come here to help rob the mayor, Ed,' Belle replied and repeated what she had already told him so that Emma would not suspect they had discussed the matter.

'How do *you* stand on it, Ed?' the blonde inquired,

158

having scanned his face worriedly all through the story.

'You-all gave me half a million good reasons for not trusting Simmy, Emma gal,' Dusty drawled and saw relief replace the anxiety on her face. 'But, knowing who she was and why she'd come, why in hell did you pick that fight with Belle?'

'I didn't know for sure, until it was too late,' Emma insisted. 'By the time I did, there were folks listening. What would they have thought, knowing *me*, if I'd done nothing after coming on some stray tail-peddler pawing at my man? And, what's more important, Simmy would have got suspicious if he'd heard I let her get away with it, even knowing she was Belle Starr. He's smart enough to starting guessing I'd got a reason for keeping friendly with her.'

'You could've let Belle know—' Dusty began.

'She did,' the lady outlaw commented dryly. 'Just as soon as I got her held down and primed for plucking, she squealed out that she'd got the other half of the bill. Then, when I held back from whomping her even uglier than she is, she cut a rusty and bucked me off.'

'You could've broke it off easy enough,' Dusty pointed out, recollecting the incident. 'All one of you had to do was make out she was licked.'

'Which one?' Emma countered. 'I didn't aim to and she sure as hell wouldn't.'

'She's right, Ed,' Belle went on. 'After it'd got that far, we had to know who's boss.'

'It was your fault!' the blonde hissed, glaring at Belle. 'You didn't have to come to my place. I'd've come and seen you later.'

'Not that it would have stopped me coming, but I still didn't know how you tied in with me,' the lady outlaw answered. 'How would it have looked to whoever had sent for me if I'd shown as such a fraidy-cat that I let a fat, blowsy calico queen back me down?'

'Just because you got lucky—!' the blonde spat, clenching her hands.

'Are you pair going to quit mean-mouthing each other and get down to horse-trading?' Dusty growled, sounding his most savage. 'Because, happen you start hair-yanking again, I'm going to chill both of your milk *pronto*, and I won't do it gentle. I'm not missing my chance of a cut in a half-million dollar pot because two blasted she-males don't like each other.'

'Don't get riled, Ed!' Belle yelped, in well-simulated anxiety, knowing that his outburst was directly mainly at the blonde. 'I'm sorry for what I said, Emma. If you'll say the same, we'll forget our quarrels.'

'You're no tail-peddler,' Emma apologized and sat down on the end of the bed. 'It's over as far as I'm concerned.'

'Let's hope you both mean it,' Dusty said, swinging his left leg over the back of the chair and settling astride its seat. 'Now I like you pair fine, and it's sure pleasing to a man's ego to have you fighting over him. But there's a time and a place for it. You can snatch each other bald-headed, or bite off your apples so you're both flat-chested once this chore's over. Until then, you'll stay peaceable.'

'We'll mind it, Ed,' Belle promised, seeing that the blonde was taking the warning very much to heart. 'Now I'd like to hear what kind of game I'm getting dealt into.'

'Simmy keeps all his money, packed in flour sacks in case he has to load up and get out in a hurry, in a cellar under his office,' the blonde explained. 'It's got a secret, trick door that only two people know how to open.'

'You're one of them?'

'No, Belle.'

'Forcing Simmy to open up won't be easy,' Dusty warned, thinking furiously of how he could turn the unexpected situation to his advantage. 'He's one tough *hombre* no matter how he acts and talks.'

'We won't have to force him,' Emma corrected. 'Giselle's going to open up for us.'

'His *wife*?' Belle ejaculated.

'And *my* half-sister,' the blonde elaborated. 'She doesn't like the way he uses her and she's sick to the guts of being buried alive in this God-forsaken hell-hole. Only she's like me, she hates going hungry. That's why we've figured this deal out.'

'Why send for me?' Belle wanted to know. 'There're

dozens of men in and out here all the time who could have helped you.'

'Do you know why I don't have a picture on my sign board?' Emma countered. 'Because you can't get a painting of something that doesn't exist.'

'*Gracias,*' Dusty drawled.

'Somehow, the Lord knows how, I get the feeling I can trust you, Ed. But you hadn't come when I sent for Belle. I needed somebody with brains enough to help me set things up, and with enough knowledge to get us away after we'd pulled the robbery. I'd always heard you're a square-shooter, Belle, so I got in touch with you.'

'Then why make the big play for me?' Dusty asked.

'We decided we could use a few real good guns to back us up if things went wrong,' Emma admitted frankly. 'Giselle was set on bringing in Ben Columbo and his riff-raff. I was sure relieved when you boys made wolf-bait of them all, Ed. And, after I'd watched you for a spell, I believed we could count on you, Matt and Comanche.'

'I get a notion this's *not* going to work out as easy as it looks from the top,' Belle remarked. 'Way I see it, we'll need a wagon to tote away all that much money—'

'The saloon could use some supplies,' Emma told her. 'And Ed owns the livery barn. Its last owner left it to him in his will.'

'It was Simmy's idea I should have the place,' Dusty explained. 'For helping him gun down its old owner and his side-kicks.'

'And, if I know Simmy,' Emma went on. 'He's already figuring out ways to get you boys killed and take it back. That's the wagon, and a reason for wanting it, fixed up, Belle.'

'There's a right good way we could pull it off tomorrow, happen you girls're up to it,' Dusty drawled.

'Tom—!' Emma gasped, darting an inquiring glance at the lady outlaw.

'I'm up to it, if you are, Emma,' Belle declared and the blonde nodded.

'How many of your crowd can you trust, Emma?' Dusty inquired. 'I mean trust all the way. With your life, because that's what's at stake if you're wrong about any one of them.'

'Hubert's the only man of 'em. Simmy hired all the others. Then there's Red, Juanita and four more of the girls. But—'

'That'll be enough, way I plan it,' Dusty insisted and went on with a comment in keeping with the character he was playing in Hell. 'We don't want to have to cut the pot too many ways, now do we?'

'If we use them,' Emma announced grimly. 'They're in for their share.'

'Why not? It's big enough,' Dusty smiled, sensing that the blonde was sincere and liking her for it.

'What's this idea of yours, Ed?' Belle inquired.

Instead of answering, the small Texan cocked his head in the direction of the window. The sounds of revelry still rolled unabated from the Honest Man Saloon.

'You sure packed them in tonight, Emma gal,' Dusty finally said.

'Just about everybody in town. I've never drawn such a crowd,' the blonde answered and threw a grin at the lady outlaw. 'If we wasn't figuring to be gone by night, I'd near on suggest that you and I lock horns again tomorrow, Belle.'

'Now it's funny you-all coming out and saying that,' Dusty put in and something about the way in which he spoke drew the girls' eyes to his face. 'I was just going to say you should do it.'

Silence followed the small Texan's words, lasting for several seconds as Belle and Emma digested the implication behind the soft-spoken, but significant words. Involuntarily, two sets of female fingers fluttered to bruised faces. Then the girls looked at each other and Dusty could see the speculation in both sets of features.

'You mean you want us to put on another cat-fight to get everybody in my place watching us,' Emma guessed. 'Then your boys, Hubert and my girls go with Giselle, load up the wagon with Simmy's money and pull out?'

'Something like that,' Dusty agreed.

'And what happens to us when he finds out the money's

gone?' the blonde demanded. 'He'll figure who must have taken it and how.'

'I've got a way around *that*,' Dusty assured her. 'Time he knows about it, we'll have a good head start on him. Only the fight's not going to take place at the saloon. You're going to have it out at that hollow on the other side of town from Simmy's place.'

I think I noticed it on the way in,' Belle remarked, nodding in satisfaction. 'Anybody out there won't be able to see Simmy's house for the other buildings in between. You've hit it, Ed.'

Emma did not join in the lady outlaw's paean of congratulation. Having been longer than Belle in Hell, the blonde knew that the hollow in question was the area set aside beyond the town limits, so that visitors could settle disagreements without endangering lives or civic property – using guns.

CHAPTER SIXTEEN

I'LL BRING 'EM BACK TAMED

Leaving his saddled *grulla* standing ground hitched by its dangling reins, Dusty Fog looked around. With the time wanting ten minutes before four in the afternoon, almost everybody in the town had already gathered at the hollow. They were all eagerly awaiting a continuation of the events which had so excited them in the Honest Man Saloon the night before. A glance towards Hell told Dusty that he had been correct about the invisibility of the mayor's house from the hollow. If careful planning and attention to detail could command success, the small Texan hoped that his work in the town called Hell would soon be at an end.

At first, on learning where he wished the clash to take place, Emma had vehemently refused to take part in it. Even Belle had been startled on being told of the purpose to which the hollow was usually put. Patiently, Dusty had elaborated on his plan and the girls had admitted that it could work. So they had discussed it at length, amending and improving, until all had felt sure that it stood a better than average chance of succeeding. Despite facing the prospect of another confrontation, the girls had parted on friendly terms. So much so that Emma had not raised a single objection to 'Ed' remaining in Belle's room for the rest of the night.

'I don't want to be a hog, Belle,' the blonde had claimed cheerfully. 'And if you feel like love-making tonight, I'll near on be willing to admit you're a tougher gal than me.'

Not that Emma had needed to worry about such an eventuality; although the reason for Belle abstaining from 'love-making' had nothing to do with her current physical condition. As the lady outlaw had told Dusty earlier, only one man had shared her bed – and Mark Counter was the small Texan's *amigo*. So Dusty had slept on the floor, which had been his intention all along.

Rising somewhat earlier in the morning than had become his habit since arriving in Hell, Dusty had left Belle and gone to find his companions. On wakening the Kid and Juanita, he discovered that Emma had wasted no time the previous night.

On her return to the saloon, slipping in by a rear entrance as unnoticed as she had left, Emma had waited until the place was closing and sent her maid to collect the Kid, Waco and the trusted members of her staff. After satisfying herself that they were all sober enough to understand what she was saying, she had told them of 'Ed Caxton's' plan. Sharing Giselle's antipathy towards the town, Hubert and the girls had stated their eagerness to leave; especially as they would do so with a sizeable stake for their futures. Before they had gone to their respective beds, they had all known the parts they would play in the robbery. Always something of a madcap, Red had been particularly pleased with the role she was selected to play.

Leaving his *amigos* to dress, Dusty had visited the livery barn and given orders for a wagon to be prepared. To lull any suspicions the bleary-eyed hostlers might have felt, Dusty had explained that the previous night's celebrations had depleted the saloon's stocks to such an extent that there was some urgency in obtaining a fresh supply of liquor.

That had paved the way for the next stage of the operation. Returning to the hotel, Dusty had escorted Belle to lunch in the crowded dining-room. Before the meal had ended, Emma stormed in. Give the girls their due, they had put on quite a performance. Screaming insults at each other, they had seemed on the verge of coming to blows. When Dusty had intervened, Belle had warned Emma that she intended to settle the matter permanently. Instantly the blonde had flung out a challenge to meet Belle at the hollow. Amidst a low mutter of excited comment from the eavesdropping occupants of the room, the lady outlaw had taken up the challenge. Mockingly saying that Emma would need time to settle her affairs, Belle had suggested they meet at four o'clock. Agreeing, Emma had stalked away.

So, at ten minutes to four, the scene was set, the audience assembled and waiting for the arrival of the principal performers in the drama. Soon after lunch, the Kid had brought word that Emma had contacted Giselle and the little brunette was ready to play her part. On visiting the barn, Dusty had found the wagon provisioned for the journey, its team hitched up, but the whole staff already on their way to the hollow so as to make sure of a good view of the proceedings. When Dusty had left in the wake of the crowd, Hell had had the appearance of a ghost town.

Elbowing his way arrogantly through the crowd, Dusty found Lampart in the forefront. The small Texan now had a part to play, one which would make a tremendous difference to the success of the plan. Glancing around and seeing a couple of the Honest Man's gamblers taking bets amongst the crowd, he believed he knew how to handle things.

'Hey, Simmy,' Dusty greeted. 'Where's Giselle?'

'She's decided not to come,' the mayor replied. 'Had too much to drink last night and's feeling the effects.'

'Sounded like you sure had a time,' Dusty grinned.

'Yes,' said Lampart coldly. 'And all free.'

'Why worry? You'll get it back and more, way they'll be drinking and talking after this. It's a pity we can't get some betting on it.'

'Can't we?' Lampart asked.

'Hell. Who's going to bet against Belle in a shoot-out?'

'You're sure she'll win?'

'I'd say it's a foregone conclusion.'

'I wouldn't,' Lampart answered. 'Emma's a damned good shot.'

'You tricky ole son,' Dusty drawled admiringly. 'Hell, though, you've made one lil mistake. Emma might be able to shoot, but I'm betting she can't lick Belle to the draw.'

'Damn it!' the mayor ejaculated. 'You're right. If—There's a way out.'

'There'd best be,' Dusty drawled. ' 'Cause Belle's coming now.'

Carrying her coat and hat, Belle walked through the crowd. She was dressed in a shirt, Levi's pants and moccasins, with her gunbelt strapped on. Behind her, ground hitched by Dusty's *grulla*, stood her powerful bay gelding. Hooves drummed and Emma, clothed in the same way as Belle but with a Navy Colt thrust into her waistband, rode up. Dismounting, she dropped her reins and followed the lady outlaw through the gap which had opened in the crowd.

'Hi Ed, honey,' Belle greeted, then jerked her head in the blonde's direction. 'Your fat slack-puller's not backed out.'

'I sure hope you got all you wanted last night, tail-peddler!' Emma replied. 'Because it was your last night in this world.'

'Yeah?' Belle hissed, crouching slightly and hooking her right hand over the Manhattan. 'Well—'

'Ladies!' Lampart barked and the girls looked at him. 'I thought this was supposed to be a fair fight?'

Concealing his grin of elation, Dusty watched the mayor do just what the plan called for. When Belle insisted that she would not have it any other way than fair, Lampart pointed out her advantage in a draw-and-shoot affair. Then he suggested that they fought as in a formal duel.

'You'll stand back to back, each holding her gun,' Lampart enlarged. 'Then I'll give the word. You each step off six strides, turn and start shooting.'

'That's all right with me!' Belle declared.

'Anyway'll do me just so I can get a bead on her,' Emma went on.

Going into the centre of the hollow, the girls stood back to back. Looking around, Dusty was satisfied that none of the crowd had eyes for anything other than Emma and Belle. Across at the other side of the circle, Waco stood between Red and a Chinese girl from the brothel. The size of the crowd caused the girl to press against his side. That too was what Dusty wanted to happen.

'If you're ready, ladies,' Lampart said, from the rim of the hollow and on receiving answers in the affirmative, continued, 'Start when I reach three. One! Two!—'

Having made a circle of the town to make sure that all was clear, the Ysabel Kid returned to the livery barn. Hubert sat on the box of the wagon and, at the Kid's nod, started the team moving. By the time they had reached Lampart's house, Juanita and the other girls were already inside.

'Move it, all of you!' the Kid ordered, looking in at the rear door.

'We already have,' Giselle answered, indicating the pile of bulging flour sacks on the floor. 'Get them loaded while I pick the locks on the deposit boxes. There's no sense in leaving their contents behind.'

'Nope,' grinned the Kid, thinking of how the losses would affect the town and its citizens. 'There sure ain't.'

'What about the guards at the shack there, Comanche?' Hubert inquired, darting a worried glance at the adobe building and remembering the men who usually stood watch over it.

'They've gone to see the fight like everybody else,' drawled the Kid. 'Go help the gals. I'll make sure nobody comes around asking what we're at.'

Sweating girls, unused to strenuous activity, darted to and fro, fetching and dumping sacks of money into the wagon. While they did so, Giselle put to use her ability as a lock-picker to unfasten the boxes in which various gang leaders had left their loot for safe keeping. Working swiftly, the girls emptied each box in turn and the brunette locked it up again. All the time, the Kid's party were conscious of a continuous rumble of noise reminiscent of the crowd's reaction to the previous night's fight at the saloon.

'We've got it all,' Giselle announced at last, hurrying out of the house.

'Don't forget that key,' warned the Kid.

'I won't,' the brunette replied. She closed the door and

left the key on the outside but did not lock it. 'I've left a note telling Simmy that I'll be down at the saloon until dinner time.'

'Will he figure anything suspicious about that?' the Kid demanded, watching the girls boarding the wagon. 'You and Emma never acted friendly.'

'It's all right,' Giselle insisted. 'Before Simmy left for the hollow, I told him that I meant to take over the saloon if Emma was killed. He'll think that's what I'm doing.'

'It'll maybe buy us some more time then,' drawled the Kid. 'Get aboard, ma'am, so's we can be going.'

With all the women in the rear of the wagon and its canopy's flaps closed, the Kid leapt astride his roan. Hubert set the team into motion, swinging them away from the street. As they reached the top of the slope, the Kid looked back to make sure they had not been observed and followed.

'Three!' Lampart finished and the crowd waited in silent expectation.

Instead of stepping straight off, Belle addressed Emma over her shoulder. Her words carried to the spectators' ears.

'Hey, slack-puller. You're lucky I'm going to kill you. After last night, Ed wouldn't waste his time bedding with a fat old whore like you.'

Letting out a shrill shriek of what sounded like genuine rage, Emma hurled her revolver aside. She twirled around, left hand shooting forward to catch hold of Belle's right shoulder. With a jerk, the blonde swung the lady outlaw to face her and delivered a slap with the other hand. There was no faking with the blow. It impacted on Belle's cheek, sending her reeling and, in part, causing her to drop the Manhattan.

Landing on one knee, Belle saw Emma rushing at her. With a yell, the lady outlaw plunged upwards, diving to tackle the blonde about the waist. Down they went, rolling and thrashing on the ground in a brawl every bit as wild as the one they had put up the previous night.

Although the crowd had come to witness a gun fight,

none of them raised objections at the way things had turned out. Prudence and caution had caused them to stay on the edge of the hollow when lead might start flying. Once Belle and Emma discarded their firearms and resumed the kind of fighting which had entertained the onlookers at the Honest Man, the crowd began to move forward. Throwing a grin at Red, Waco contrived to keep the Chinese prostitute at his other side.

Walking to the waiting horses, Dusty watched the people moving down into the hollow. Lampart was going with them. Despite his gamblers having money wagered on the result, he could not resist the temptation to sample once more the erotic delight of watching two beautiful women embroiled in primitive conflict. Everything was still going as the small Texan had planned.

Dusty had realized from the beginning that a gun fight, even if its result could be faked, would not last for long enough to let the robbery be carried out and the wagon disappear over the rim of the crater. So he had told the two girls how to act. Belle's reference to Emma as a slack-puller – which, like tail-peddler, meant a whore of the cheapest variety – and comment about the previous night had been sufficient to bring the blonde's reaction without arousing the spectators' suspicions.

'Come on, Lon!' Dusty thought. 'Get things moving!'

If the Kid and his party had set to work as soon as possible, they ought to be coming into view soon. The longer the delay, the greater chance of something going wrong. Lampart might become aware of the ammunition guards' presence in the crowd and order them to return to their post.

There was the wagon now!

Good for Lon and Hubert. They had remembered their orders and hidden the girls in the back of the wagon. Trust Lon to restrain any urge the bartender might show towards making the team go faster. If anybody should happen to see the wagon ascending the slope, there was nothing about it to hint at a hurried, illicit departure. However, the leisurely pace also had its disadvantages.

While Belle and Emma were aware that they must keep

their fight going for long enough to let the wagon's party escape undetected, things could go wrong. In the heat and excitement of the tangle, tempers might easily be lost and one or the other knock her opponent unconscious. So far, from all Dusty could see and hear, they were carrying out their assignment in a satisfactory manner.

At last, after what seemed a far longer period than it had actually taken, the wagon disappeared amongst the trees. With a long exhalation of relief, Dusty hung Belle's jacket and hat – handed into his keeping by the lady outlaw before going out to take up the duelling position – on her saddle. Vaulting afork his *grulla*, he gathered up the other horses' reins and set the three animals into motion. Riding on to the slope, he caused a hurried scattering of spectators anxious to avoid being ridden down. On reaching the front of the crowd, he saw that he had not come too soon.

With fingers interlaced in matted, sodden, dishevelled hair, Belle and Emma knelt clinging weakly to each other. Their shirts had gone and they looked to be close to collapsing through sheer exhaustion. Leaping from his saddle, Dusty stalked forward. Silence fell over the crowd as they watched and wondered what the small Texan planned to do. Reaching the girls, he bent and gripped their back hair in his hands. Drawing the heads apart, he snapped them together with a hard, crisp click.

'What the hell?' Lampart barked as Dusty released the girls' hair and they crumpled in a heap at his feet.

'If these two bitches wanted to shoot it out, it was fine with me,' Dusty replied, bending again and lifting Belle from Emma. Holding the lady outlaw in his arms, he continued his explanation while walking towards the horses. 'That way, I'd've been shut of one or the other. I'll be damned if I'm going to have them keep cat-clawing each other over me. Neither's fit to bed with when she's through fighting.'

'But what are you planning to do with them?' Lampart insisted, watching Dusty heave Belle belly down across her saddle.

'I'm going to take 'em off aways, just me and them,' Dusty explained and went to collect Emma. With the blonde draped limply over her horse's back, he went on. 'Comes night, I'll bring 'em back tamed.'

'But – But—!' Lampart spluttered, wondering how he could turn the small Texan's actions to his own advantage.

Slowly Dusty walked over and retrieved Belle's Manhattan. A low mutter rose from the crowd, querulous in its timbre if not out-and-out hostile. Straightening up, he stuck the revolver into his waistband. Hooking his thumbs into the gunbelt, he swung around and left a descent of silence where his eyes had passed over.

'Anybody who objects can step right out and say so,' Dusty declared. 'Only he'd best come to do it with a gun in his hand.'

There was no reply. Everybody present knew 'Ed Caxton' as the feller who had simultaneously out-drawn two of the fastest gun hands Hell had ever seen, then made wolf bait of a slew of other bad *hombres* who had crossed his trail. If any member of the crowd should accept the challenge, that man would die almost as soon as he mentioned his intentions. In every male mind – except possibly Lampart's – lurked the same summation. They had seen a mighty enjoyable cat-fight. One which, way the contestants had been looking during the last few seconds, would have tamely ended in a draw through them both fainting from exhaustion.

So why get killed over it having been stopped?

'Ed Caxton' sounded like he aimed to keep both girls around. One thing was for sure if he did, they would be unlikely to grow friendlier. So, for all his proposed 'taming', there was always the chance that they would lock horns again. In which case, the wisest thing for every man present to do was let that big Texan tote them off – stay alive himself, and wait to see what the future held.

Seeing that he had made his point, Dusty mounted his *grulla*. He rode up the slope, leading the two horses and their inert burdens. Lampart watched him go, thinking fast.

'Didn't some of you fellers have money bet on who won?' the mayor inquired as Dusty rode over the edge of the top of the hollow.

At the words, Waco gave Red a nudge with his hip to warn her that she must play her part. Excitement glinted in her eyes. Springing by the youngster, she confronted the Chinese girl.

'You quit a-pawing my feller, you slit-eyed whore!' Red shrieked.

'What you speak, round-eye calico?' the Chinese girl spat back, for there was no love lost between the prostitutes and Emma's employees.

'I'll show you what I speak!' Red promised, conscious of being watched by both factions.

Ducking her head, Red leapt at and butted the Oriental in the chest. Reeling backwards, the girl sat down. Another of the brothel's contingent made as if to attack Red. That did it. Already brought to a pitch of wild excitement by the fight between Belle and Emma, the two factions needed no more urging. Squeals and yells rose, then that section of the crowd exploded into a multiple tangle of hair-pulling, fist-swinging, screeching females.

'You started th—!' the brothel's bouncer began, moving towards Waco.

Before the words ended, the blond youngster's fist took the man under the jaw and knocked him from his feet. Like the ripples spread by throwing a stone into a pond, the fight developed until it engulfed every member of the crowd. Even Goldberg's plump, pompous wife joined in, mixing it as gamely as any saloon-girl with her husband's partner's younger, prettier spouse.

A good ten minutes went by before Waco found himself close to Red. In that period, the fight had become general and a matter of attacking the nearest person of the same sex. Red sat astride Mrs. Goldberg and the jeweller's wife, pounding indiscriminately at both while they continued to settle old scores. Grabbing the girl by the hair, Waco hauled her bodily clear of the mêlée. When she tried to turn on him, he first slapped, then shook her into a more pacific frame of mind.

'That's better,' Waco growled, carrying her up the slope. 'I'll take you back to the saloon and you can get into something you can travel in.'

'Wh – When do we g-go?' Red gasped, brushing away her tears.

'After I've done a lil job for Du – Ed,' Waco replied.

Fortunately, Red's exertions had left her in no state to think clearly. So she did not notice the blond youngster's mistake. Clinging to him, she pressed her bruised, scratched face against his shoulder.

'What's the lil job?' the girl asked. 'Is it important?'

'Enough,' Waco answered.

The blond did not explain how if he succeeded in his 'lil job' he would most likely save the lives of many people – or that the penalty for failure was even more likely to be death.

CHAPTER SEVENTEEN

MISS NENE, MEET CAPTAIN DUSTY FOG

'Howdy, Simmy,' Waco greeted, strolling along the sidewalk to where the mayor was unlocking his front door in a decidedly furtive manner.

Lampart looked anything but his usual, neat, immaculate self. Unable to slip away before the general brawl had entrapped him, he had been compelled to fight back until he had dropped to the ground and feigned unconsciousness. By the time he had finally escaped, leaving the battle still raging, he had lost his hat, jacket and cravat. His torn shirt looked as if it had been walked on – and had. It had been his hope to reach his home without anybody seeing him, for he knew there would be those who wanted to know why he had done nothing to end the conflict. Although the street was clear, that blasted blond youngster had come through the alley and surprised him.

'How did you get here?' the mayor demanded ungraciously.

'Same's you. I got out soon's I could.'

'So it seems,' Lampart growled, glaring at Waco's unmarked features and all too aware of his own injuries. 'What do you want?'

'Some money out of our box.'

'Can't it wait?'

'Sure. Happen you don't mind the chance of the saloon getting damaged.'

'Huh?' grunted the mayor.

'I sure's hell don't aim to stay away from it,' Waco explained. 'And there could be them's reckons Red 'n' me's to blame for that ruckus at the hollow. So I conclude buying drinks good 'n' regular ought to change their minds. Talked to your lady down there, and she claims I've got a right smart notion.'

'My wife's at the saloon?'

'Why sure. Taking on like she owns it.'

That figured to anybody who knew Giselle, the mayor mused. From what she had been saying when she had heard about the gun fight, his wife had expected her half-sister to be killed. So she had not waited to hear the result before going to assert her control of the saloon. One thing was for sure. No matter who ran the Honest Man, its profits – and losses – descended on Lampart. What young 'Caxton' said was true, too. After a night without a drink being sold – although many were consumed – due to that blonde bitch's boastful stupidity, Lampart had no desire to incur further losses.

'Come in and get what you need,' the mayor ordered, wanting to get off the street as quickly as he could.

With which sentiment Waco heartily concurred. Nobody had seen him meet the mayor. Even Red was unaware that he had, having gone to her room to change ready for their departure. That made the blond youngster's task just that much safer.

'I allus got the notion Ma Goldberg and that fancy young wife of the jeweller's didn't cotton to each other,' Waco commented cheerily as Lampart took him inside and locked the front door. 'They sure was whomping each other all ways when I lit out.'

'She always blamed Melissa for Goldberg getting caught out,' the mayor answered, opening up his office. 'I should have one of the Regulators here—'

'You've got one,' Waco pointed out. 'Me. You made me one after we'd got rid of ole Basmanov's bunch for you.'

'Of course,' Lampart grunted and waved his hand towards the boxes. 'Help yourself.'

'*Gracias,*' the youngster drawled, walking by the desk. Scooping the Colt from it, he turned and threw down on the mayor. 'Only I've changed my mind.'

'You've done what?' Lampart spat, staring at the Peacemaker as it lined on his chest.

'Changed my mind,' Waco repeated, thumb-cocking the revolver. 'So, if you'll open up that drawer with the "magnetic" battery in it, I'll touch off your ammunition supply and head for home.'

'Home? With a price on your head!'

'Shuckens, that's not worrying me one lil bit.'

'Do you reckon that the Army will forget what you've done just because you've got rid of my ammunition?' Lampart sneered.

'Just what have I done?' Waco countered.

'Helped to kill a colonel, sergeant and six men,' the mayor reminded him.

'You shouldn't believe all you read in the newspapers, Mr. Mayor,' the blond youngster drawled. 'Those fellers're no closer to heaven – or hell, I'd say in Paddy Magoon's case – than down to the OD Connected.'

'The—?' Lampart gulped.

'The OD Connected. That's our spread. Me, the Ysabel Kid – and Dusty Fog's.'

'Dusty Fog?' croaked Lampart.

'Yes sir, Mr. Mayor,' Waco confirmed. 'My "Brother Ed's" Dusty Fog. Now open that drawer, or I'll do it myself.'

'Can you?' Lampart challenged.

'I can give it a whirl. This room's pretty thick-walled. I could burst the desk open without making enough noise to be heard outside of 'em.'

'You've a point,' Lampart admitted sullenly, hanging his head in dejected fashion. He walked around and sat behind his desk. Without looking at Waco, he opened the required drawer with his left hand. 'Here you are.'

For all his beaten aspect, Lampart was grinning inwardly. In addition to having been a successful stage illusionist, he was also a skilled maker of magical tricks and gadgets. Being aware of the type of people with whom he would be dealing, he had put his inventive genius to work in Hell. Not only had he fitted a secret door to the cellar which held his wealth, but he had equipped the desk with a protective mechanism. The latter had already proved its worth.

On their last night alive, Glover and Eel had not meant to return to Hell. So their use as a future source of revenue had ended. They had not attempted to draw their guns until he had shouted the unnecessary warning – and by that time it was too late. In fact, he had even been compelled to pull out Eel's weapon to make his story ring true. Fortunately, Cowper had been close enough to the building to hear the shots. Rushing in to investigate, holding his gun, naturally, he had died at 'Ed Caxton's' hand.

Except that the *big* Texan was not 'Ed Caxton', if the blond youngster was telling the truth. He was Dusty Fog and he had come with his two companions to destroy Hell.

Which raised the question of why Fog had sent the young blond to handle the dangerous task of blowing up the *Kweharehnuh's* reserve ammunition supply.

Most likely the blond had asked to do so, as a means of winning acclaim and, probably, higher financial rewards. Judging the Rio Hondo gun wizard by his own standards, Lampart decided that Dusty Fog would be only too pleased to let another man take the risk. Whatever had happened, the blond was going to pay for the rash, impetuous offer with his life.

Still keeping his head bowed, so that no hint of his true feelings would flash a warning to his victim, Lampart rubbed his left foot against the inner support leg of his desk. A click sounded and a section of the desk's top hinged up close to his left hand. Out of the hole exposed by the section rose a block of wood. On top of the block rested the ivory-handled Webley Bulldog which had taken Basmanov's, Glover's and Eel's lives. Scooping up the weapon, he lifted his eyes to Waco's face and a mocking smile twisted at his lips.

Ever since organizing the escape of so many badly wanted criminals, Lampart had felt a growing sense of his own brilliance. He had brought Hell into being, arranging for it to become the lucrative proposition which it now was. With each achievement, he had grown more certain that no lesser man could equal his superlative genius, or defeat him in a match of wits.

Fog and his companions might think they were clever, but Lampart would teach them differently. There was no need for haste, not even in dealing with that impetuous young fool who stood before him. He wanted to see the other's expression on pulling the Peacemaker's trigger when only a dull, dry click rewarded the gesture. The appearance of the Bulldog would have been a severe shock, but the failure of the Colt would be even worse.

So Lampart moved in an almost leisurely manner – and paid the penalty.

Instead of trying to fire the useless Peacemaker, Waco had drawn his left hand Army Colt as soon as the section of the desk began to move. Flame ripped from the eight inch barrel as the Webley was lifted from its resting place. Hit in the head, Lampart slammed back. Tipping over under his weight, the chair deposited him on the floor. The Webley slid unfired from his lifeless left hand.

'Dusty was right,' the youngster breathed, placing the Peacemaker on the desk and darting to the window which overlooked the street. 'Knowing about that old plough-handle did help to save my life.'

Even before Dusty had touched the revolver and found it was too cold to have been fired, he had suspected that some other weapon was responsible for Glover's and Eel's deaths. The shots had been fired too quickly for a single action even being fanned. Which meant that the mayor had another firearm. It was not on his person, so it must have been concealed in the desk. Confirmation for the suspicion had come from the examination of the bodies. If Glover had been pointing his revolver at Lampart, his forefinger would have been in the triggerguard. A man with the outlaw's experience, however, would have known better than to place his finger on the trigger until the barrel had left the holster and was pointing away from him.*

Having heard Dusty's warning, Waco had turned his own thoughts to the matter and come up with further con-

* Why is told in *The Fast Gun*.

clusions. One clue had come from Dusty's description of Lampart's ambidextrous card manipulation. Considering that, the youngster had decided the mayor had used his left hand when firing the hide-away gun. The cocked Peacemaker would be there to distract his victim. Carried a stage further, Waco had decided it was unlikely that the Colt would fire. It would be too easily available to an enemy – as his own actions had proved – for a *hombre* as smart and tricky as the mayor to chance having it capable of being turned on him with live ammunition in the cylinders.

So Waco had never intended trying to defend himself with the borrowed Colt. Instead, he had gambled on his own ambidextrous ability and had won.

Looking along the street, the youngster decided that the shot had not been heard. He returned his Colt to its holster as he went to the desk. Taking hold of Lampart's body, he dragged it to a corner so that it could not be seen from either window. With that done, he went to examine the contents of the open drawer. A sigh of relief burst unbidden from his lips. The 'magnetic' battery was there, coupled up and ready for operation. It was one of the portable variety designed to supply an electric current for use with a mobile telegraph station. Bent had one just like it at his place in the Indian Nations and, ever curious about unusual things, Waco had learned how it was worked.

On Waco throwing the activating switch, there was a deep roaring bellow from behind the house. The adobe shack disintegrated in a sheet of flame and billowing black smoke. Even in the mayor's office, Waco could feel the blast and concussion of the explosion shake the house. Glass shattered as windows broke and he heard shouts of alarm rising. Darting from the office, he locked its door and pocketed the key. Then he sprinted through the living quarters. Giselle had followed Dusty's orders to the letter – trust ole Lon to see to that. Going out he found the key in place in the rear door. He turned, removed and pocketed it. Then, as the first of the people attracted by the commotion appeared, he began to shake at the door.

'What happened, Matt?' demanded an outlaw whose face carried marks from the battle at the hollow.

'I'm damned if I know,' the youngster replied. 'That blasted blullet-shack just son-of-a-bitching went up.'

'Where's Lampart?' the jeweller demanded, looking around. 'I've warned him that this might happen, keeping that blasted fuse wired up.'

'Door's locked,' Waco replied. 'Sombody'd best go around the front.'

Men dashed to do so, returning with the news – which did not surprise Waco – that there was no sign of the mayor or his wife.

'I'll tell you one thing,' Waco yelled. 'I'm not waiting around to find out where he is. When the *Kweharehnuh* hear there's no bullets coming to 'em, they're going to get mean. Comes that happening, I figure to be long gone.'

With that, he pushed through the crowd and headed for the livery barn. Red was waiting, dressed in Levi's pants, a blouse and dainty hat.

'What hap—?' the girl began.

'Don't talk, mount up and ride,' Waco interrupted, indicating the horses which stood saddled and ready. 'We've got some miles to cover afore we catch up with the others.'

Three days later, the united party made camp a few miles north of the Swisher Creek's junction with the Prairie Dog Fork of the Red River. They had come that far without difficulty, other than that suffered by Belle and Emma. Although each claimed that she had held herself in check all through the second fight, both now had two blackened eyes and so many additional bruises that they could not ride their horses.

On being questioned about the explosion, Waco had told the truth without revealing his companions' true identity. He had said that he considered his actions were for the best. Destroying the ammunition would cause even the outlaws whose boxes had been looted to be more concerned with fleeing from the Palo Duro than in pursuing their party. Giselle had taken the news of her widowhood calmly, declaring that she was relieved to know that she need never worry about Simmy tracking her down.

Waco's summation had proved correct, for nobody had come after them. They had seen one group of

Kweharehnuh warriors, who had ridden by without stopping. Indicating a distant column of smoke, the Kid had guessed that it rose from the Antelopes' village and was calling the various parties of braves in for a conference about the destruction of their ammunition.

A couple of the town's guides had approached the party. On hearing what had happened in Hell and discovering that their presence was unwelcome, they had ridden away. When last seen, they had been heading east as fast as their horses would carry them.

After supper, while Waco was hoorawing the Kid for having forgotten the excuse which it had been arranged that Giselle would use to prevent her husband suspecting she had left town, Dusty asked Belle and Emma to join him for a stroll. They were in safe country at last and the time had come for certain matters to be settled. Once out of earshot of the others, the blonde raised the very subject which Dusty had meant to introduce.

'When do we share out the loot, Ed?' Emma asked.

'That's what I asked you both out here to talk about,' Dusty admitted.

'What's to talk about?' Emma demanded. 'We just sit around the fire and go, "One for you". "One for you". "One for you", until it's all split up even.'

'Not quite,' Dusty objected. 'You stop going "one for you" when you, Belle and Giselle have fifty thousand apiece and the girls and Hubert have ten thousand each.'

'There's well over half a million in the pot, Ed,' Emma said coldly. 'I'd say you and your boys're taking a kind of selfish split.'

'Not when you consider we've got to share it with all the banks it came from,' Dusty countered.

'B–Banks—' Emma spluttered and swung to the lady outlaw. 'Do you know what the hell he's talking about?'

'Yes,' Belle replied. 'I think I do. He's giving us a reward for helping him finish off a chore.'

'Now I don't know what the hell *you*'re talking about,' Emma groaned. 'Unless you're in cahoots—'

'You might say we are,' Belle smiled. 'And before you start something we'll both of us regret, I reckon I should introduce you to this feller you've been fighting me for.'

'Intro—!' Emma yelped. 'I know who he i—'

'Miss Nene, meet Captain Dusty Fog,' Belle interrupted.

'Is—' the blonde finished, then her mouth trailed open and she stared at the *big* Texan. 'D–Did she say *Dusty Fog*?'

'That's what she said,' Dusty confirmed.

'Then you're not Ed – You've been using me!'

'No more than you were willing to use me,' Dusty pointed out, studying the play of emotions on the blonde's face. 'I was sent by the Governor to close Hell down and, with you folks' help, I've done it. Now this's my deal. You-all take the cut I've just offered and go with Belle. She'll see you safe through the Indian Nations to Kansas. And you've got my word that I'll not say a thing about you being part of the town.'

'It's a good offer, Emma,' Belle remarked. 'And seeing that we've no other choice, I reckon we'd best take it.'

'You're not Ed Caxton!' the blonde breathed, eyes fixed on Dusty and showing no sign that she had heard the lady outlaw. 'You're—I've slept with Dusty Fog!'

'Stop your bragging just because you've done something I haven't,' Belle suggested with a smile.

'You mean that you and E–D – nothing happened last night?' Emma gasped, showing she had heard Belle's last comment.

'Dusty slept on the floor like a perfect gentleman,' Belle declared. 'How about it, Emma, do we take Dusty's offer? If not, I took a lot of lumps for nothing.'

'I reckon fifty thousand dollars ought to make up for them,' Emma replied. 'You're calling the play, E–D – Captain Fog.'